FOLLOW YOUR HEART

When Ruby Byrne and her children emigrate to Canada in 1920, love is the last thing she expects to find. But when widower Robert Kerr proposes, she is happy to accept. Cait is pleased for her mother, yet she can't help thinking about her former fiancé, Trevor Thomas, back in Cardiff. Robert's son, Martin, is determined to win Cait as his bride, but is it fair to marry him when Trevor is still in her heart?

CATRIONA McCUAIG

FOLLOW YOUR HEART

Complete and Unabridged

LINFORD
Leicester

First published in Great Britain in 2009

First Linford Edition
published 2010

British Library CIP Data

McCuaig, Catriona.
  Follow your heart. - -
  (Linford romance library)
  1. Immigrants- -Canada- -Fiction. 2. Welsh
  - -Canada- -Fiction. 3. Love stories.
  4. Large type books.
  I. Title II. Series
  813.6–dc22

  ISBN 978–1–44480–341–9

Published by
F. A. Thorpe (Publishing)
Anstey, Leicestershire

Set by Words & Graphics Ltd.
Anstey, Leicestershire
Printed and bound in Great Britain by
T. J. International Ltd., Padstow, Cornwall

This book is printed on acid-free paper

1

Have you ever considered how easily your world could change in an instant, for better or for worse? You can be plodding along, minding your own business, when, unknown to you, the fates are busy making plans to turn your life upside down. Cait Byrne certainly had no notion of what lay ahead in the next few weeks when she set out to meet Trevor Thomas on that Sunday afternoon in Cardiff in the spring of 1920.

The couple been going out together for some time and they had settled into a comfortable routine. Cait thought how pleasant it was to be holding his arm as they walked up past the castle and headed for the banks of the Taff River. Anyone could see they belonged together!

Cait's head was packed full of

romantic notions after having attended her best friend's wedding. Bursting with enthusiasm she described to Trevor as they walked all that had happened there, the previous day.

'I wish you could have been there too, Trevor. I did think that Mary might have asked you, but it was such a small affair; just a few of us at the registry office, you know. The reception afterwards was just a matter of tea and sandwiches at her home. There was barely enough room for everyone to sit down as it was. I was the only person there who wasn't a family member, and that was only because I was her bridesmaid.'

She paused for a moment, remembering the radiant bride, and the groom in his shiny suit, a look of pride on his face. Poor Tom had lost an arm in the war but his Mary had stood by him and they couldn't have been happier if they were wealthy socialites instead of two young people with only a few shillings to their name.

'They'll be as poor as two church mice but they're so lucky and so much in love,' she concluded softly.

'It will be our turn one of these days,' Trevor said, as they stared down at the slow-moving water. 'I mean, you do know that I will want to marry you one day, don't you, Cait?'

She turned to face him. 'I'm not sure that I do. Oh, you often say that sort of thing in passing but you haven't actually proposed to me yet, Trevor, not properly, really.'

'I suppose girls always want something romantic, with flowers and soft music and all that,' he said, rather embarrassed. 'And you shall have that, Cait, when the time comes. I'll do it properly when I'm in a position to get engaged, but for now I'd just like to make sure we both feel the same way and want to stay together.'

'Of course I do, but why do we have to wait? I know it might be some time before we can marry, but couldn't we announce our engagement? As long as I know you love me I wouldn't care about all the trimmings.'

'Then will you marry me, Cait? I love you with all my heart,' he said, moving to take her into his arms in full view as she blushed happily.

'Well, really!' A stout matron wearing a faded frock in the pre-war high-necked ankle-length style, trimmed with jet buttons, glared disapprovingly at them as she passed.

Cait giggled as Trevor released his hold on her. 'We won't be getting engaged until I can afford to get you a ring,' he said firmly.

'Never mind that. I don't need one, Trevor. The money could be put to use in better ways, like saving up for the furniture we'll need for our new house when we get married.'

'No, Cait, we'll do this properly or not at all. You deserve a ring, and a lovely ring you shall have!'

Men could be so silly at times. Fancy thinking that she needed a ring on her finger before she was prepared to give

4

her heart into his safekeeping! Knowing that Trevor loved her, and that some day she would be his wife, was worth more than all the diamonds in the world!

'But it doesn't need to be expensive,' she murmured. 'Something pretty from a second hand shop. Honestly, I don't mind at all.'

But Trevor had made up his mind and that was that! Cait smothered a sigh. She and Trevor had been walking out for two years now, with walking being the operative word, because they had little money for outings. Both of them were trying to save money, but it wasn't easy.

Cait had to help out at home of course. Her mother often said that she wished she didn't have to take so much out of her daughter's pay packet but it couldn't be helped. Cait's father was dead and his family had to manage as best they could. Naturally Cait was glad to make her contribution to the household.

Trevor was in a similar situation. He

worked as a clerk in the dock offices and, after handing over most of his salary to his widowed mother for his keep, there was hardly anything left over. It was unkind really because Mrs Thomas was supposed to be quite well off, but she was often heard to remark that she despised spongers. Cait had a nasty idea that the woman liked to keep her son under her thumb.

And that was another thing! Trevor had taken her home to tea a couple of times now, and Cait had the distinct impression that Mrs Thomas believed that her one and only son could do better than a girl who worked in the Post Office!

Of course, their two mothers were a generation apart. Mrs Byrne had married young, while Mrs Thomas had produced Trevor much later in life. Cait guessed her prospective mother-in-law must be almost 70.

'I wonder where they're going to live, your friends,' Trevor mused.

Cait came to with a start. 'Oh,

Mary's parents have redecorated her bedroom for them, I understand.'

Trevor nodded. Many young couples had to start married life in one room in a parent's home. Cait shuddered at the thought. Some people said that two women sharing one kitchen was a recipe for disaster. Not so bad when the other woman was the bride's mother, but how difficult would it be for a new wife to fit in with her mother-in-law's ways?

Cait would most definitely prefer not to share with Trevor's mother, which was another reason for needing a bit a money behind them. Perhaps it was just as well if they kept their plans secret for the moment, although naturally she would tell Mam that at long last they were semi-engaged.

'I suppose I'd better be getting back now, or Mother will start to get worried,' Trevor said. 'But I'll see you get back home first, of course.'

As she trotted along beside the man she loved, Cait was once again lost in a dream in which she and Trevor played the starring roles. The couple she had witnessed exchanging their vows yesterday had seemed so confident of a happy future together, despite the fact that they obviously hadn't a penny to bless themselves with.

Now it seemed to be a foregone conclusion that she and Trevor would be meeting at the altar at some time in the future. She felt as if she was about to burst with happiness.

If only they didn't have to wait so long! Never mind, she told herself, she would just have to be patient and some day she would have her reward. It would be all the sweeter for having had to wait.

★   ★   ★

'I'm just nipping over to Frank's, now, Mam,' Danny Byrne put his head round the sitting room door, putting his arm into the sleeve of his coat as he did so.

'All, right, dear. Have you given your shoes a good polish? You mustn't let Frank down at his wedding rehearsal!'

'Yes, Mam!' Danny knew his mother meant well, but he felt impatient with her at times. After all he was a twenty-four-year-old man, and a veteran of the Great War. He didn't need reminding as if he was still a schoolboy! He had known Frank Sharpe since they were boys in the Mixed Infants and now he was to be best man at his wedding. How the years had flown by!

He took a quick look at himself in the hall mirror, liking what he saw. His navy blue suit had been well brushed by Mam, and he was sporting a clean white shirt and a new tie. Not that Frank would notice; he would have eyes only for his lovely bride.

Frank greeted Danny with enthusiasm. 'Here you are, then, boyo! I can't believe that the big day is almost here at last!'

'Neither can I!' Danny retorted. 'When I think of the grubby little urchin you used to be, I wonder that any woman would take you on. Your Elsie must be mad, that's all I can say!'

Frank punched his friend on the arm. 'Even more remarkable, she's willing to let me have you for my best man, which is certainly not the action of a sane woman!' They laughed and went into the kitchen, where Frank proceeded to make a cup of tea, saying that he needed a pick-me-up to calm his nerves.

'It's just as well you're getting married soon,' Danny said seriously. 'I don't think I'll be hanging around this place much longer, Frank.'

'Not leaving Cardiff, are you? You've always said you love the old place. Even when we were boys you used to say you'd never want to live anywhere else.'

'Nothing wrong with Cardiff, as such; it's me. The war has changed everything. I can't settle down to civilian life somehow. The thought of spending the rest of my days selling socks and ties, and going back home at night to share a room with that lazy young brother of mine, leaves me cold. There has to be more to life than this!'

'It seems pretty good to me,' Frank said softly. 'After losing most of my friends in the fighting on the Somme I was surprised to find myself still in the land of the living when the guns stopped. It's a mystery to me how I managed to survive when they didn't. All I want now is a quiet life with a wife and family. As for a dull job, I'm glad to have one. Every time I see those poor wounded chaps sitting in the arcades with their caps in front of them hoping for a penny or two, or standing in the rain with a tray of boot laces for sale, I tell myself how lucky I am.'

'If I'd served in the trenches I might feel the same way you do,' Danny replied, 'but it was different in the Royal Flying Corps. You don't know what it feels like to fly, soaring above the clouds like a bird and seeing the world far below; that same old world we were fighting to preserve. It's glorious, Frank.'

'And deadly dangerous,' his friend said soberly. 'You were up there to kill or be killed, just as we were, down on the ground.'

'Do you know, I actually caught a glimpse of the Red Baron one day,' Danny went on. 'I once heard him described as a worthy adversary, probably the greatest air ace ever known, although he was only twenty five when he died. He chalked up eighty victories before they finally got him. Few pilots survived long enough to even come close to a record like that.'

Frank nodded. Everyone had heard of Manfred von Richtofen and his Flying Circus. The German hero was known as the Red Baron because his aircraft was painted red.

'Mam doesn't understand when I talk like this,' Danny went on. 'I'm certainly not glorifying the war, or making little of the sacrifice of those pilots who were killed in the dog fights. It's just that once you've learned to fly, it's hard to get it out of your system.'

'And having to spend my days selling clothes for other fellows to wear has brought me down to earth with a bit of bump.'

'So what do you plan to do?' Frank was really concerned now.

'I've all but made up my mind to have a go farming in Canada.'

'Whatever gave you that idea?'

'Surely you've seen all the advertisements in the newspapers? The Government is recruiting people to take up farming in the Canadian West. People are flocking there from all over Europe, it seems, so why shouldn't I join them? I'd be eligible for more than a hundred acres, all free, except for ten quid to register the deed in due course.'

Frank stared at him, open-mouthed. 'It sounds too good to be true. What do you know about farming? You're a townie, born and bred.'

'If I can learn to fly, I can learn to farm,' Danny retorted, smiling. 'Everyone has to start somewhere. Come to think of it, why don't you and Elsie come with me? It'll be a grand life in the wide open spaces.'

Frank's mouth twisted bitterly. 'No thanks! I saw all the countryside and mud I'll ever need when I was in the army. Well, good luck to you, Dan! If it doesn't work out you can always come back, I suppose.'

'No fear! Onward and upward, that's my motto!'

The blare of a horn warned them that their taxi had arrived, and Danny shepherded his friend outside, saying they mustn't be late in case the bride arrived before them and changed her mind. That was hardly likely, of course. Danny was pleased to see his old friend looking so happy and contented. Elsie seemed like a good sort, and Danny hoped they'd have many happy years together.

Later, he found his sister at home, ironing a blouse she wanted to wear to work the next day.

'How did the rehearsal go off? It seems that everybody is getting married these days. What about you, Danny? Isn't it time you thought about settling down?'

He looked over his shoulder, obviously uneasy. 'I want to show you something, Cait, but don't tell Mam, all right?'

'What is it? You know she doesn't like us keeping things from her.'

By way of reply he handed her a letter to read. 'I've had this from Martin Kerr, in Canada. You've heard me speak about him. We were in the Flying Corps together. I wrote to him recently and, well, I suppose I moaned on a bit about finding it hard to get used to civilian life again. The long and short of it is, he thinks I should go out there, to Canada.'

The letter seemed sensible enough and Cait came to the conclusion that going abroad might be just what her brother needed to rid him of his discontent. The Kerrs lived in a small Ontario town called Kildare, and Martin's father had generously offered to let Danny stay with them until he could find his feet.

'He can always use an extra hand on the farm if you're worried about taking advantage,' Martin had ended by saying. 'That would give you a chance to see if you're suited to farming before you burn your boats and head West. As to that, a lot of fellows from here are doing the same thing, so you'd be in good company.'

Cait was impressed. 'So why not give it a try, Danny? Even if you had to accept the same sort of work over there as you're doing here, at least you'd be in exciting new surroundings. And if you don't take to it you can always come back home.'

'I'd go in the blink of an eye, but there's just one problem. It's Mam! She won't like it, and not only only that, I wouldn't feel right about leaving her to struggle on with one less wage coming in. It'll take all my savings to pay for my passage, so there'd be nothing left over to help her out.'

'But now's the time to go, don't you think? I mean, you don't have a wife and children to think of. You're footloose and fancy free.'

* * *

'You're going to do what?' Ruby Byrne's normally quiet voice sounded shrill as she glared at her eldest child.

'I'm going to Canada, Mam. There's nothing for me here any more.'

'That's great! Can I come with you?' his young brother Mickey piped up. His mother turned on him, furious.

'You be quiet, Michael Byrne! Who asked for your opinion? As for you, Daniel, I'm cut to the quick to hear you say there's nothing here for you!' Ruby held her clasped hands to her breast as she tried to blink back the tears. 'What about your poor mother, and the rest of the family, then? Are we not important to you any more?'

'Now, Mam, you know I didn't mean it like that. It's the job. It's leading nowhere. I'm healthy and single and I've no ties as such. There's nothing to hold me back, that's all I was trying to say.'

'Then look around for something else. Surely you don't have to go thousands of miles away from home to find something better?'

'But chances like this don't come along every day of the week. Think of it, all those acres of land, all for nothing.'

'Huh! Nothing in this world is free, Daniel Byrne! And even if this land is handed to you on a plate, you'll need plenty of other things if you hope to go farming. Horses and ploughs, for instance. And what about furniture, and food to tide you over until you get money from your first harvest? Have you thought of all that?'

Danny's mouth set in a stubborn line. 'I have savings, Mam,' he said.

'Then why not wait until your annual holiday is due? With the money you have put by you can afford to travel anywhere in Britain and see what the prospects are.'

Cait sent an uneasy glance in her brother's direction. Mam was talking to him as if he was still a little boy, not a grown man who had played a brave part in the war! Couldn't she see it was putting his back up? What neither of them realised, of course, was that Ruby Byrne, like every other mother who had been involved, had suffered agonies when her son was away at the war. She wanted to cosset him now she had him back at last, and instead he was talking about going to the other side of the world, where who knew what dangers lay in wait.

Danny was not an unkind young man. 'Listen, Mam,' he said. 'I won't be going among strangers, as you seem to think. I had a letter from my pal Martin today and he tells me I'd be welcome to stay with his family for a while when I first go out there. He'll be going home on holiday soon and he'll take me to meet people who can answer my questions about farming in Canada. Now, won't that set your mind at ease?'

'I suppose so,' Ruby began, 'but oh, I wish your father was here to help us thrash this out. Wait a while before you make a move?'

Danny shook his head. 'If I'm going at all, I need to get organised at once. I can't see any point in waiting until winter comes. My savings would soon dwindle if I had to pay for lodgings during bad weather.'

Ruby's mouth tightened. She was going to have a fight on her hands but she wasn't about to give up without a struggle!

2

Hurrying through the streets of Cardiff, Ruby Byrne wanted to be in good time for work. There was a haze in the air that spoke of a hot day to come but for the moment it was cool. She would have liked to linger, to gaze into shop windows and to exchange greetings with women who were outside, scrubbing their front steps.

She loved the old city where she had been born and brought up. A Welshwoman through and through, she had married Barney Byrne at the age of 17, captivated by his good looks and Irish charm. He, too, had been born in the Valleys, for over the years many Irish people had migrated to Wales, hoping to find the work that wasn't there at home.

Ruby reached the small green grocery where she worked six mornings a week. Old Mr Raymond had already pulled down the canvas awning in anticipation of the sunny day ahead, and was now busily stacking wooden boxes of fruit and vegetables on a table outside, where they would attract the attention of passing trade.

Unusually for him he failed to greet her and she went inside to take off her coat, wondering what was up. When she emerged from the cubbyhole at the back of the shop, pulling her striped apron over her head as she came, she found him inside the shop, looking glum.

'Anything wrong, Mr Raymond? Mrs Raymond is all right this morning, isn't she?'

His wife suffered from arthritis and was slow to get started in the morning, which was why Ruby worked here until after the lunch hour trade had slowed down.

'She was well enough when I came downstairs,' he muttered, raising his eyes to the ceiling as if he could see his wife in the upstairs flat. 'The thing is, Mrs Byrne, it's bad news in a way. We've decided to sell up. We're neither of us getting any younger and we've had a good offer, see? We've decided to take it and move to Bristol to be near our daughter. She's been on at us to go ever since my wife had that fall back in the winter.'

'I see,' Ruby murmured, 'but that's good news, surely?'

'For us, I suppose, but the thing is, the new owners have a family, and they'll all be working here in the shop. Big plans for expansion, they have, if they can get hold of the empty premises next door.'

Light dawned. 'So what is it you're trying to tell me, Mr Raymond? I'll be out of a job, is that it?'

He nodded. 'I'm afraid so. There's sorry I am, Mrs Byrne, but there's nothing I can do. I did put in a good word for you, but they've got it all worked out. Why pay when their own family will work for nothing?'

Why, indeed, Ruby thought. She could hardly blame the Raymonds for wanting to retire, but where did this leave her? There weren't many jobs going for women in 1920. During the war it hadn't been so bad; women had been needed in the factories, taking the place of fighting men, but once the Armistice had been signed they were expected to return to their kitchens! All right for some, but Ruby was a widow with very little money to spare.

Luckily her children were more or less grown up and she was able to make ends meet by running a little dress-making business at home, assisted by her daughter, Cait. Unfortunately that didn't pay all the bills. People would only pay so much for sewing, not taking into account the many hours it took to make a frock or a skirt. Thank goodness for the treadle sewing machine!

'Mr Raymond has given you the news, I suppose?' Mrs Raymond had hobbled downstairs at the usual time to tell her husband his dinner was on the table. An appetising smell of liver and onions wafted into the shop in her wake.

'Yes, he did, Mrs Raymond. You'll be happy in Bristol, I'm sure.'

'He'll give you a good reference, I know. I expect you'll find something else in no time.'

Ruby doubted that, but she nodded pleasantly as she shrugged on her old cloth coat. No chance of a new one this spring, then!

'You can take some of them apples — the cookers, mind, not the eating kind — and p'raps you'd like a nice fresh cauli.' Mrs Raymond smiled. 'That'll go down a treat in a nice cheese sauce, that will.'

Ruby smiled back as she pulled her string bag out of her pocket and began to fill it with apples. Getting free fruit and veg was one of the perks of the job, which she would miss almost as much as the work itself. The Raymonds had a reputation for selling the best of everything and would not dream of putting spoiled fruit on display. Anything that was slightly past its best at the end of the day was taken upstairs for their own use, or shared with Ruby.

Then she set off for home, trying not to worry too much about the future. As she always did when things went wrong, she thought of her dear husband Barney, who had died when their children were still young. What would he have said about her present troubles? 'Worse things happen at sea!' he'd have said, with a cheeky grin. Barney was one of nature's optimists. How she missed him!

As for her job, she could afford to take her time looking around for something else. There was bound to be something.

In the meantime, things could have been worse on the home front. All of Ruby's children were in work. Danny had a good job in a gentlemen's outfitters, Cait seemed well established at the Post Office, and even her youngest son was earning now. If she could ask each of them to hand over a fraction more of their wage, just temporarily, of course, they'd be able to manage. Young Mickey would complain bitterly, no doubt about that, but at 15 he had a tremendous appetite and it cost a lot to feed him. It was only right that he should contribute to the household.

'Prynhawn da, Mrs Byrne!' Ruby's neighbour hailed her from an upstairs window as she turned into Marley Street and got to her door.

'Prynhawn da!' Ruby answered as she fumbled for her latchkey.

'Have you heard the news, Mrs Byrne? There's terrible it is!'

For a moment Ruby thought that Elsie Jones was talking about the shop changing hands. Then she realised that the woman must be talking about something different.

'What news, Elsie? War hasn't broken out again, has it?'

'Na, na, but this is worse. They're pulling down this street and that's no word of a lie! Jenkins the milk told me, and he got it from his boss at the dairy, him that's on the council.'

Ruby could hardly take it in. 'Pulling it down! But whatever for?'

Elsie shrugged. 'Who knows? Cos they want to build something else I suppose. And Marley Street isn't the only one, apparently. A whole lot of streets are slated for demolition.'

'But what about us? Where will we go?'

'Your guess is as good as mine, bach! All I can say is, we'd better start looking around for something else before the rush starts.'

A querulous voice from inside caused Elsie to withdraw her head. She lived with her old father and he was now demanding attention. Stunned, Ruby fitted her key into the lock. First her job, and now this! Hardly aware of what she was doing she went to put the kettle on. She needed a cuppa. A strong one!

★ ★ ★

Mickey Byrne was a sore trial to his mother. In some ways he took after his father, being a happy go lucky sort of boy who seldom worried about anything. The difference was that Barney Byrne had been responsible where it counted, whereas any criticism rolled off their youngest son like water off a duck's back.

Mickey had left school at the age of 14 and now worked as a grocer's boy, pedalling around the streets on his delivery bicycle, taking people's orders to their homes. Ruby had a terrible time getting him out of bed in the mornings, especially on wet days, when he moaned and burrowed under his blankets.

'Michael Byrne! You get down these stairs this very minute!' she bawled, failing to get a response. It was a Monday morning and her older children were already up and about, gulping down their breakfast before leaving for their own work.

'Danny, would you mind going up

see what's keeping him, please? I've called him till I'm blue in the face, and it hasn't made a bit of difference!'

'I already told him to shake a leg, Mam, for all the good it did. You should just let him lie there and face the music when he turns up late for work. I've told you that before. It's the only way he's going to learn.'

'He might lose his job then, and with me in the same boat I'm not prepared to risk it. He may not earn much, but we need every penny. You go up and see to him, Cait, there's a good girl.'

'Only if I can take a wet sponge with me,' Cait muttered. 'That boy will come to a bad end if he doesn't mend his ways soon.'

Ruby was inclined to agree. Was it her fault? Had she spoiled Mickey because he was her last baby, born seven years after the rest of them? She had lost one baby at six months and Mickey had seemed like a gift from heaven. Perhaps she hadn't disciplined him as she should.

With a slice of bread and jam in one hand and a well polished apple in the other, Mickey wandered out into the cold morning air, bleary-eyed and disgruntled. Work was boring and he wished he didn't have to go. School had been bad enough but at least you could mitch off from time to time, even if it did mean the cane when they caught up with you. Not much chance of doing that now, not if he wanted to keep his job.

'You're late, Byrne!' Mr Sutton growled. 'That's happened twice this month already, boy! This is your last warning, mind!'

'Yes, sir. Sorry, sir.'

'Now you've finally decided to honour us with your presence, you can get started on them orders. There's a big important one for the Lilacs in Carmarthen Road, and on the way there you can drop off a pound of tea to the Misses Llewellyn at the old manse. With the amount of tea those two drink, I don't know why they don't buy more of it at one time, and save my poor old legs. If I cross this shop floor once in a day I must cross it a thousand times.'

'Your poor legs! What about mine on that heavy old bone shaker?' Mickey muttered under his breath, not daring to answer back where the boss could hear him.

He cheered up somewhat when Miss Llewellyn offered him a rock bun to keep his strength up, and by the time he reached the big house which was next on his route he had regained his usual good humour.

He carried the shopping to the side door and was surprised when nobody came in answer to his knock.

'Delivery! Anybody home?' But still nobody appeared so he shrugged and set the box inside the little porch. This was a nice neighbourhood and the things should be safe enough until the cook came back from wherever it was she had gone.

Back at the shop he was put to work

dusting the shelves in the store room and, after checking over his shoulder to make sure that the boss wasn't in the vicinity, he pulled his *Boys Own* paper from out of his pocket and began to glance through it. Before long he was engrossed.

'Byrne!' It wasn't often that Mr Sutton roared like that, so Mickey rushed out to see what was wanted. Mr Sutton was holding the telephone receiver away from his ear to avoid the indignant squawking coming from the other end of the line.

'Just one moment, Mrs Jenkins, if you please.' He turned to deal with Mickey, his nostrils flaring.

'That is the cook at the Lilacs. She wants to know why her order hasn't arrived. What have you done with it, boy?'

'I delivered it, sir, just like you said. There was nobody home so I put it in the porch. Tell her to look out there. She'll find it, all right.'

Mr Sutton hung up the telephone ear

piece and turned to face Mickey, who by now was quaking in his hob-nailed boots.

'There is no porch on the back door of the Lilacs, boy! Worse than that, the lady needed some ingredients for a cake recipe, items that she had ordered from me and which I was glad to supply. Expecting to receive these at any moment, she had already started working with what she had at hand. She'd already cracked open the eggs and it all went to waste when the ratafia and the demerara sugar failed to arrive.'

'Oh, dear.'

'Yes, indeed. Now, if memory serves me correctly, there is a porch on a house called the Cedars, farther up the road. I suggest you get up there as fast as your legs will carry you, and find that missing parcel and deliver it to its rightful owner!'

Mickey scuttled off and did as he was told, but his troubles weren't over. A maid at the Cedars told him loftily that 'we don't deal at Sutton's!' and when he finally met the cook at the Lilacs she said a few things which made his ears burn.

'And we'll be dealing with Mackin & Jones in future so you needn't bother coming here again,' she snapped, by way of a parting shot.

When she started out for home shortly after six o'clock, Cait was amazed to find Mickey skulking behind a bakery wagon that was drawn up across the street from the Post Office where she worked. She was late leaving because she'd been in the sweet shop next door, where she'd just spent an agonising five minutes trying to choose between pear drops and buttered brazils, and she had crossed the street to pet the horse, who happened to be a favourite of hers.

'Mickey Byrne! What are you doing here without your delivery bike? You're miles from where you should be at his time of day!'

'Nothing,' he mumbled, scuffling the toe of his boot in the dry dust.

'There is so!' she retorted, moving a buttered brazil into one cheek, the better to get the words out. 'I bet you've got the sack, and serve you right, too,' she gloated, with sisterly candour.

'Ssh!' he whispered, looking past her fearfully. 'I don't want Mam to find out. According to her getting the sack is almost as bad as going to prison. She'll never get over the disgrace.'

'She'll know soon enough,' Cait said, taking pity on him and thrusting the sweetie bag towards him. 'Don't take more than one, mind. I know you, Mickey Byrne! Like I said, she'll know what's happened when you don't go to work tomorrow morning.'

'I'm going to leave home each day the same time as usual so she won't be able to guess.'

Cait raised her eyes to heaven. 'You are an idiot, Mickey! What are you going to do when it comes time to tip up your pay packet?'

He looked at her with misery in his eyes. 'Don't know. I haven't thought that far ahead yet.'

'My advice to you is to confess right away and get it over with,' she advised. 'Why suffer when you don't have to?'

'I'll suffer all right when Mam catches up with me,' he muttered.

'Oh, Mam won't kill you,' she told him, linking arms with him and attempting to pull him along. 'Come on, home we go! All for one and one for all.'

As they marched through the busy streets Mickey gasped out his story piece by piece. 'It was all the fault of that cook at the Lilacs,' he grumbled. 'If she hadn't complained to the boss everything would have been all right.'

'You must have done something, surely?'

'There's mean you are, Cait. I thought you'd stick up for me!'

'I will. I am sticking up for you. I just want to know what happened.'

Mickey's freckled face tightened into a scowl. 'If you must know, I delivered the order to the wrong house. I took it to the Cedars instead of the Lilacs down the road. Cedars, Lilacs; they're all the same to me.'

'Is that all? Anyone can make a mistake. Why didn't they just ask you to go back and switch them over?'

'Tell that to old Sutton! 'We have built up a reputation for absolute accuracy and reliability',' Mickey warbled, mimicking his employer, ''and I can't keep an employee who cannot meet our high standards'.'

'Ouch! Never mind, I'm sure our Mam will understand.'

'I hope you're right,' Mickey said gloomily, 'but somehow I doubt it. With two of us out of work. We'll be eating bread and scrape all week.'

3

When Cait and Mickey reached home it was to hear raised voices coming from the kitchen.

'I tell you, Mam, I can't stick it much longer! I'll go mad if I have to keep working in that beastly shop with old Williams criticising my every move! Today he blew his top because I'd put a grey shirt on the shelf with the blue ones. As if it mattered!'

'I hope you haven't been giving in your notice, my lad!'

'I haven't yet, but the writing is on the wall. Can't you see, Mam? Canada is my only chance and I'd be a fool to pass it up!'

Tip-toeing into the kitchen Cait heard him say something about a marvellous opportunity and the chance of a lifetime. There was no smell of cooking in the room and no sign of anything waiting to be popped into the oven.

'What's for tea, Mam?' Cait seized her chance during a lull in the conversation.

'Bread and scrape!' her mother retorted. 'I've had no time to think about meals, not after the bombshell this brother of yours has dropped on me. After all I've said he still insists on sticking to this foolish idea of going to Canada, and he's ready to give in his notice at work!'

Cait was dismayed by the look of strain on her mother's face. 'Why don't we go for fish and chips, then? When we've eaten we can sit down and talk this over calmly. We'll all feel better once we have some food in our stomachs.'

'All right,' Ruby agreed, reaching for her shabby purse. 'Bring hake if they have it, and make sure they put plenty of vinegar on the chips. And mind you don't start gobbling the food until it's on the table here, Mickey Byrne!'

Back home again, Cait removed the

pages of newspaper from the steaming package of food and smoothed it out carefully while Mam placed heated plates on the table. Nothing was ever wasted in this household and newspaper was useful in many ways.

A long letter attracted her attention and she paused to read the first few lines before folding the page and placing it in her apron pocket. When the last delicious morsel of food had disappeared and the small amount of washing up had been disposed of she brought it out again and waved it in her mother's direction.

'What is it, dear? A new dress pattern?'

'No, Mam. It's a letter from somebody in Canada, telling how well things are going with him and encouraging others to emigrate.'

'Here, let me see that!' Danny reached over to grab the sheet and Cait held it behind her back where he couldn't get at it.

'I saw it first, Danny Byrne! I tore

this out for Mam to see.'

Silently, Ruby read the letter before passing the paper over to her son. 'This man makes it all seem very nice, I must say, but is it to be believed? I expect he was asked to write it by those colonisation agents, or whatever they call them. They want to encourage lots of people to go out there, so I don't suppose they'd want to let any letter of complaint appear in print, would they?'

Danny looked up from the letter with shining eyes. 'This sounds good to me, Mam. Look here, he does say that hard work is needed if prospective settlers are to succeed in Canada and that's fair enough. I'm quite prepared to work, and once I get on my feet I'll send for you all to come out and join me. It'll be a fabulous new life for all of us.'

Mickey sat up straight in his chair. This was wonderful! Danny was his hero and he could think of nothing better than to be with him in this new venture. On top of everything else, the opportunity could not have come at a better time for him.

Ruby felt a pang as she glance round the room at her family assembled there. She was always at her most contented when they were all together, and she couldn't bear the thought of being separated again from her firstborn after getting him back safely after the war.

Suddenly, she came to a decision. 'Very well, Daniel Byrne,' she said bravely, 'you make what arrangements you must, but you needn't think we're staying behind while you go to some foreign country on your own! You're to wait until we can find the money for the passage, and then the rest of us will come with you. We have to move from here in any case, so we may as well go to Canada!'

She looked around the shabby room to gauge her family's reaction. Danny looked elated, Mickey seemed filled with excitement, and Cait . . . well, there was a steely look in Cait's eye-which her mother had never seen before. 'The rest of you can go if you like, but I'm staying put! if you think I'm going thousands of miles away from my Trevor you're very much mistaken!'

Ruby's jaw dropped. Seizing his opportunity, Mickey jumped into the breach. On the theory that it was best to get all the bad news out in the open at once, he explained how and why he'd been given the sack.

'Oh, Mickey! How could you be so stupid!' she bawled, but could tell her heart wasn't in it. She was more concerned with Cait's ultimatum. They were so busy arguing the toss that nobody noticed when he slipped out of the room.

★　★　★

'Stop that, young man! The noise is enough to wake the dead!'

Mickey scowled up at the irate housewife who was blocking his path. He had been wandering aimlessly, head down, kicking a tin can in the gutter as he went.

'Sorry,' he mumbled, although he failed to see what all the fuss was about. What with fog horns blaring and all the usual sounds of city traffic his little effort didn't count for much. Still, that was women all over; always grumbling about something.

'If you don't find yourself a job soon, my lad, we'll be in the poor house!' his mother had complained, when she'd returned to the attack later. 'You'll start looking first thing in the morning, although who will take you on when you've just been sacked I don't know.'

'I thought I'd have a bit of a holiday first,' he muttered.

'A holiday! Your life is one long holiday, boyo! Well, you can stay in bed for a week for all I care but you needn't think you'll be getting the sort of meals you've been used to! Food costs money, and that commodity is in short supply at the moment.'

In vain Mickey tried to explain that it only made sense for him to have time off now while he had the chance. 'I haven't had a holiday since I started at Sutton's and when I do get another job that'll be it; no time off for the first year.'

'Oh, dear, then I'd better send you to Barry Island for a week, all expenses paid!' Ruby sniffed, and it was a moment or two before he realised that she was joking.

'If we don't go to Canada, p'raps I could go to sea, like Dad did,' he told her. 'That would set me up for life, that would.'

Cait had laughed, not unkindly. 'Don't I remember you being sick on the ferry when we went to Weston with the Sunday School treat? I can just see you sailing round the Horn, leaning over the side all day long.'

So now he was trudging from shop to shop, being told there were no vacancies. He even enquired about work on the docks, but the man in charge told him to come back when he was two years older and a good deal heavier than he was now. He didn't say there was no work for puny 15-year-olds, but Mickey could tell that was just what he was thinking.

'Byrne! What brings you here?' Mickey's heart sank when he realised that it was Mr Harrison, one of his old teachers from the board school. The man was standing beside a mobile tea wagon, munching a sausage roll. 'Not in work, then?'

Mr Harrison had always had a down on Mickey, or so it had seemed at the time. He seemed to have a fund of unkind things to say, calling the boy an idle lout who would come to no good. His remarks were uncalled for; Mickey certainly had a lazy streak but he had always been honest and truthful. No son of Ruby's could have been anything less. Now, though, the fibs poured from his lips as he was determined to tell old Harrison a thing or two.

'I've given in my notice,' he said proudly. 'I'm going farming in Canada with my big brother. We're going to get acres and acres of land, and get rich.'

'Are you, by jove!' The school master looked at Mickey through narrowed eyes. This sounded like a tall tale, yet, like everyone else, he had been reading the appeals in the newspapers and knew that large tracts of land were still available to anyone willing to go out to the Dominion. Whether there was a pot of gold to be found in those acres was something else again, but stranger things had happened.

'Well, my boy, I do believe there are great opportunities for young men in the outposts of the Empire,' he said, using the lofty language which had characterised his classes at the school. 'When do you leave for Canada?'

'Nothing is settled yet, sir.' Mickey was on safer ground now. 'My brother is looking into it, but we hope to leave before long because we need to be out there before winter sets in. They have a lot of snow in Canada, you know.'

He marched on, whistling cheerfully, leaving Mr Harrison staring thoughtfully at his retreating figure. When he'd rounded the corner the boy slowed down, feeling guilty. He hadn't actually told any lies, though, had he? And if he had, it had been worth it to see the expression on old Harrison's face! Absolutely priceless!

* * *

Friday might be the end of the work week as far as some fortunate people were concerned, but many others were only free on Sundays. Most office workers were expected to work three Saturday mornings out of four, and school boys had to turn out for games. Those who worked in the shops had to remain behind their counters until six o'clock, begrudging every minute. On this particular Saturday Trevor Thomas trudged home moodily, wanting to save the tuppenny bus fare. He couldn't remember when he had felt so down hearted.

His mother called out to him when she heard his key in the lock.

'How did it go today, dear? Did you manage to get that promotion you were hoping for?'

Evelyn Thomas paused in the act of pouring a second cup of tea for her friend, Maudie Taylor. Her son shook his head glumly.

'I'm afraid not, Mother!'

'But I understood that Mr Simpson was retiring, and that everyone would be moved up a notch.' She turned to her friend, explaining that Mr Simpson was the chief clerk in Trevor's office.

'And so he did. There was a little reception for him today, and they presented him with a carriage clock. As we expected, Mr Bowles, the deputy clerk now takes his place, but that's as far as it goes. As you know there had been talk of each us moving a step up the ladder and a beginner hired for the bottom rung, but that turns out to have been a bit of wishful thinking on someone's part. A man has been brought in from the branch office to take over Mr Bowles' old job, and the rest of us will have to stay just as we are.'

Mrs Taylor clicked her tongue sympathetically. 'Never mind, Trevor, there's always next time.'

'Maybe so, Mrs Taylor, maybe so. The trouble is, I was really hoping for the raise that would have gone with the promotion, and of course that hasn't materialised. I'm saving hard to get married, so I need every penny I can lay my hands on. Cait is saving up as well, but as a woman she makes even less money than I do, so I'm afraid we'll be old and grey before we manage to stagger down the aisle.'

The ladies laughed at this witticism but it was quite obvious that he was badly disappointed.

'I can't say I'm sorry,' Evelyn whispered, when her son had gone upstairs to change. 'He's only twenty-five, you know. There's plenty of time yet for him to be thinking about marriage. I'd just as soon he waited a while, and looked around a bit.'

'Do you not like his young lady, then?' Maudie whispered back.

'Oh, she's a very nice girl, I'm sure,' Evelyn replied, in tones that left the impression that Cait might be nice enough for some people, but that her boy could certainly do better. 'You know, Maudie, we've been friends since we were in the infants' class together, haven't we?'

'Yes, of course we have, dear. And I've been very grateful for that.'

'So when I had Trevor, and a year later you had a little girl, I thought it would be perfect if they were to marry some day. Your Ruth has turned out to be a lovely girl, one I'd love to welcome into the family.'

'Thank you, dear; but you know, we can't force the children into marriage. They have to go their own way.'

'Yes, but it won't hurt to give them a little push. At the rate Trevor's savings are going it will be years before he can afford to get married, especially if I put my foot down and say the pair of them can't live here! Anything might happen in that time, don't you think?' She smiled, looking like the wolf masquerading as Little Red Riding Hood's grandma.

Maudie laughed. 'Great minds think alike,' she murmured. 'Of course, I can understand that you'd want to keep him with you as long as possible, especially as he was able to stay with you all through the war. 'You were luckier than most, dear. When I think of poor Mrs Hamilton up the street, losing her two sons, I want to weep.'

'I never thought to hear myself say this,' Evelyn mused, 'but Trevor having that accident when he was a boy turned out to be a blessing in disguise. He was too lame to be accepted for army service. Besides that when people noticed the way he limped there was never any thought of giving him a white feather for cowardice because he wasn't in uniform. Some even thought he must have been wounded on active service.'

As a little lad Trevor had been knocked down by a brewer's dray and had his leg broken. While he hadn't received any life-threatening injuries the leg hadn't been properly set and although he certainly couldn't be described as a cripple, he had been left with a pronounced limp.

People seldom noticed this small handicap because of his pleasant manner and quiet way of speaking, and more than one girl had fallen under the spell of this dark-haired young man, although he was far too modest to realise this. Evelyn Thomas had taken note of this, however and, proud mama that she was, felt that her boy could take his pick of any girl in Cardiff!

'Wouldn't it be lovely if we had grandchildren to share some day?' she murmured now, and her friend nodded.

'That would be the icing on the cake, indeed it would!' The two women fell into a happy dream in which they were already getting out the knitting needles, in celebration of this additional bond between them.

Trevor had a pretty shrewd idea of

what his mother was thinking. She certainly hadn't been properly sympathetic towards him! He looked forward to hearing what Cait had to say about it. She was a sweet-natured girl who would be sure to understand.

Unfortunately Cait was looking for sympathy herself. As soon as she saw him coming she broke into a run, and flung herself into his arms.

'Oh, Trevor, you'll never guess what's happened!'

'You know I'm no good at guessing games, Cait.'

'Well, you know Danny's been wanting to go to Canada.'

'I know. You've said. Surely that hasn't upset you? He's a grown man. He can surely make up his own mind about where he means to spend the rest of his life.'

'You're not listening to me, Trevor! He's going ahead with his plan, and Mam and Mickey are going with him. I'm staying behind.'

That got his attention. 'What on

earth do you mean, Cait? Why would your mother want to leave Britain and start all over again at her age?'

'Mam is only forty five, Trevor, although don't you dare mention that I told you that! And she says she may as well go, because everything is falling apart here. If Danny is going to farm he'll need somebody to keep house for him, and we all hope that this will be the making of Mickey. You know how irresponsible he is.'

'But you won't be going with them, then?'

'Of course not! Do you think I'd leave you?'

'I'm glad to hear it, but where will you live? Surely you won't want to stay on in Marley Street on your own?'

What was the matter with Trevor today? He seemed to be in a daze!

'Well, hardly! The whole street is due to come down soon. I've told you that. It's the last straw as far as Mam is concerned, and that's mainly why she's decided to emigrate. I expect I'll have to find a bedsitter somewhere.'

'A bedsitter! You'll do no such thing! A young woman of your age, living alone? What on earth would people think?'

'About the same as if I'd stayed on in Marley Street,' Cait snapped. 'I suppose there are boarding houses where I could find a room.'

Now there was silence. This was Trevor's cue to sweep her into his arms declaring that they'd bring their plans forward and get married at once. When nothing of the sort happened, she decided to give him a nudge in the right direction. 'Unless you can think of anything else?'

'What's that? Oh, no, a boarding house is your only option. It'll cost money, though. You won't be able to put much aside now, if anything.'

'We could get married before Mam leaves,' she ventured. 'That would solve all our problems, wouldn't it?'

'Don't be silly!'

Cait lost her temper. 'What's so silly

about that? We could find a room somewhere — that bedsitter you were so scathing about — and we'd be happy as could be. I know it wouldn't be easy, but we'd be able to manage somehow, surely?'

'This is the most ridiculous thing I've ever heard. For one thing, we wouldn't have your salary because they don't allow married women in your job. It was different during the war when women had to take the place of men at the front. Now the men have come home — some of them at least — and women can go back to their old lives.'

'In the kitchen, where they belong.'

'Exactly.' Either Trevor failed to hear the bitterness in her tone, or he chose to ignore it. 'And what if a baby came along before we were ready to support a family? Have you thought of that?'

'But when your raise comes through . . .'

'No, Cait! I found out today that it's not going to happen.'

'I'm so sorry.'

'Are you? Are you really? Or are you

just put out because I refuse to go along with your silly idea?'

Tears sprang into Cait's eyes. 'That's not fair, Trevor! You're the one who's being difficult here. You could at least take a moment to consider my suggestion instead of treating me like a naughty child.'

'Hardly that, old girl, but someone has to see sense in this situation.'

'Oh, yes? I'm beginning to think that you don't want to marry me at all, Trevor Thomas. It's Mummy, isn't it? I know she's never liked me.' As soon as the words were out she knew she shouldn't have spoken so rudely, but by then it was too late to take them back.

'I'll thank you to leave my mother's name out of this, Cait! If all you can do is to insult her, I suggest we postpone this conversation until you're calmer!'

'Oh, don't be so pompous!' Cait glared at him and walked off up the street without looking back.

Ruby looked up from her sewing as the front door banged open.

'Is that you, Cait? Did you have a nice walk with Trevor?' She broke off when she saw her daughter's angry expression.

'Don't bother asking, Mam!' Cait growled, her eyes flashing. 'No, we didn't have a nice time, and no, he didn't get his raise, and no, we're not getting married, now, or at any time in the future!'

'So if Danny hasn't booked our tickets yet, he'd better get an extra one, because I'll be coming to Canada with you. And don't ask me where I'll find the money because I've got enough in the bank. Why spend it on pots and pans and fancy tablecloths?' Ruby held out her arms as her daughter began to sob.

4

'Where's Mam?' Danny, leaning over the ship's rail, was enjoying himself mightily. Being tossed up and down on the rolling waves was almost as good as flying. He felt free as a bird, and happier than he'd been since the war ended.

'Still in her bunk, as sick as a donkey!' Cait muttered.

'Never mind. Only two more days and we'll be back on dry land. It only takes six days to cross the Atlantic now, not like the old days of sailing ships, when you could be at sea for two months.'

'I shouldn't mention that to Mam, if I were you! You're likely to get your head chopped off. That's if she could find the strength, poor dear!'

Danny grinned. 'She'll soon cheer up when we get to Canada.'

But below decks, in the cramped cabin that Ruby and Cait shared with two spinster school teachers, Ruby was quite sure they'd been mad to leave Wales. It was all very well for Danny; he was a young, single man who could make his way anywhere, but what was she supposed to do?

Danny assumed that she and Cait would run his home for him, while the farm supported them all, but that seemed like a pipe dream now. It was all very well to say that the government would give them acres and acres of land, but what about all the tools and equipment he'd need to run it? His savings wouldn't go far. And if she and Cait decided to go out to work, would there be jobs available? It was all very worrying.

She cheered up when the captain announced over the address system that they were entering the Gulf of St Lawrence. The sea was calm now, and they were able to go on deck, to marvel at the sights along the shore. Here and there small churches could be seen, their steeples gleaming silver in the sunlight. Neat houses, seemingly made of wood, stood far apart from each other, roofed in various colours.

At last they docked at Quebec City, where the ship would stay briefly before sailing on to Montreal, where they would disembark. Cait stared up at the magnificent stone building that towered high above them, decorated with turrets like some medieval castle. 'That's the Chateau Frontenac,' a passing steward remarked, on hearing her gasp.

'I didn't know they had old castles in Canada,' Ruby told him.

'It's a hotel, Madam, built by the Canadian Pacific Railway company, and actually it's less than thirty years old. Of course, Quebec City has been here for over three centuries. They'll be letting us off for a few hours. You should go and take a look around.'

'And I thought Canada was a young country,' Ruby murmured, wishing

63

she'd paid more attention to history lessons at school.

When at last they docked at Montreal she was thankful to have her sons with her, as they struggled to get their trunks to the railway station. There were no raised platforms as such, and steps were let down to assist the travellers to board the train. Even the carriages were different; no compartments such as they were used to back home, but arranged like buses, with long rows of seats on each side of an aisle.

Mickey sat back happily as the conductor made his way down the carriage, shouting 'all aboard!' This was the life!

'Can I get a sandwich, Mam?' he begged, seeing a red-jacketed man approaching with a tray of refreshments, suspended from his shoulders with leather straps.

'Perhaps, if they're not too expensive,' Ruby agreed, thinking that what she needed was a strong cup of tea! 'We've got to be careful with our bit of cash, son.'

But Mickey was one of those fortunate people who lived only for the moment. Tomorrow could take care of itself! However, even he was tired and cross by the time their three-hour journey came to an end, and when his brother explained that they must now change to a small, local train for the rest of the way to Kildare he had to blink back the tears.

'Cheer up, son,' Ruby told him. 'Won't be long now, and I'm sure the Kerrs will have a nice meal waiting to welcome us when we get there.'

'I'm too tired to eat,' he mumbled.

Ruby had to laugh. 'The day you turn down good food, my lad, there'll be white blackbirds!'

But even she sagged with exhaustion when they found themselves standing in front of the small station, surrounded by their luggage, with nobody else in sight in the gathering gloom. The little train had steamed away, and the station agent had gone to his house, after touching his fingers to his peaked cap.

'I thought we were being met,' Cait wailed, exhausted now. 'You said that Martin would be here to pick us up, Danny. What's going on?'

'That's what he said in his letter.'

'He must know what time the train gets in! And don't tell me we're early. That train had only two speeds, stop, and slow!'

'There must have been some mix-up. If all else fails we'll have to walk.' Ruby sighed, taking charge. 'We'd better put our trunks inside and get started before it gets too dark.'

'But we don't now where to go,' Cait pointed out. 'Oh, I wish we hadn't come! This is all your fault, Danny Byrne!'

'Now, now. None of that!' Ruby snapped. 'It's not the end of the world. Go on, Danny. I'm sure the station agent can give us directions.'

Then they heard the sound of horses' hooves coming ever closer.

'Mafeking is relieved, I think!' Danny said cheerfully, heading towards the gate at the edge of the station yard.

Mickey gave a cheer, while his mother and sister patted their hair into shape and smoothed down their wrinkled skirts.

Cait took a good look at the young man who was deftly handling the reins of a sturdy roan mare. Perhaps not as handsome as her Trevor, but a very welcome sight, nonetheless! He scrambled down from the wagon, putting out a hand to steady the lighted lantern, hanging from an upright post, as he came.

'I'm Martin Kerr,' he announced, doffing his old felt hat as he came. 'And you must be Mrs Byrne! Welcome to Canada! Have you been waiting long? I'm so sorry, but there's been a bit of a problem at home.'

'Nothing too serious, I hope?' Ruby asked.

'I'll tell you all about it as we go. Now, let's get your baggage loaded, shall we? You take the other end of this trunk, Dan, and we'll have her sorted in no time at all.'

Seated on the hard wooden benches, while the wagon jogged along, Ruby thought that her bottom would never be the same again. After all that sea sickness she could have sworn that she'd lost a few pounds, and she wasn't as well padded as she used to be. After those two train journeys, and now this, all she wanted to do was to lie on her stomach and never move again!

'So what has happened at your home, Martin?' she asked, determined to be polite, no matter how uncomfortable she might be.

'Oh, Dad fell off a ladder in the barn. He was going up to the hay loft when a rung broke under him, and down he came.'

'Oh, no! I hope he wasn't badly hurt?'

'Fraid so. Only a broken arm, though. We thought at first he might have broken a few ribs, but old Doc Harmon took a look at him and said no, just bruising. A broken arm's no joke, but it could have been worse.'

The horse began to pick up speed so Ruby surmised that they must be reaching the end of their journey and sure enough, they were soon flying along a long lane, leading up to a large brick house. The little party got down stiffly, yawning and stretching after the journey.

The door was flung open, letting a flood of light into the yard. A short, plump woman stood framed in the doorway, her hands held out in welcome. 'Well, here you are at last! You must be that tired, the lot of you. Don't just stand out here, taking root! Come in! Come in!'

'I'm Jeannie Kerr,' she went on, as Ruby stepped inside. 'Martin's Grandma, of course. And you're Ruby. And this must be your girl, and the young lad. And you'll be Martin's pal, Danny. Sit down, sit down and make yourselves at home. You must be starved. I'll dish up as soon as Martin comes in from seeing to the horse, but I daresay you'll want a bit of a wash first. I'll take you up to your room in a minute.'

No response seemed to be needed, so Ruby let the talk flow over her.

'Now then, I'll just light this,' Mrs Kerr went on, taking an oil lamp from the shelf, and you can carry it up for me. 'Cait, isn't it?' Cait nodded. 'And you'll need hot water.' She took an enormous kettle from the woodstove and poured the contents into an enamel jug. 'Now, then, ladies, off we go!'

Ruby and Cait found themselves in a low-ceilinged room, containing an enormous brass bed, covered in a colourful quilt. A carved wooden washstand held a large china bowl and matching jug. 'I'll leave you to it, then,' Mrs Kerr said, smiling. 'The towels are on the rack there. Come down as soon as you're ready and I'll dish up.'

Back downstairs again, the room was delightfully cosy, warmed by the heat of the woodstove. There was a delicious aroma of hot food, and Mrs Kerr beamed as she stirred something in an iron pot. The long wooden table, large enough to accommodate more than a dozen people, was laid with willow-pattern plates, and little glass dishes holding homemade pickles and relish.

When the Byrnes had taken their seats, Mickey reached out for a bread roll, and stuffed it into his mouth, oblivious to his mother's frown.

'Perhaps you'll ask the blessing, Martin,' Jeannie Kerr remarked, just as Mickey reached out for a second roll. Ruby glared at her younger son, who pretended not to notice.

Then Mrs Kerr filled up a plate with beef stew, mashed potatoes and green beans, handing it to Martin, who in turn passed it to Ruby.

'Don't wait for the rest of us, Mrs Byrne,' his grandmother directed. 'I abhor cold stew. And help yourself to what's on the table, do. Everything here comes from the farm, so it's all wholesome.'

'Thank you. It looks delicious,' Ruby told her.

'Cor, you can say that again!' Mickey whooped. 'We'll eat like this every day when we get to our farm, won't we, Mam?'

Embarrassed, Ruby turned to their hostess. 'How is your son, Mrs Kerr? I hope he's not in too much pain.'

'Call me Jeannie.'

'And I'm Ruby.'

'Well, he's tucked up in bed at the moment, and Doc Harmon's given him some knock-out drops, so he should be all right until morning. No doubt he'll not be best pleased when he comes to and sees his arm set in plaster. Still, better than being a cripple for the rest of his life.'

'Is it far to the hospital? Was it a long journey?'

'Bless you, no! The nearest is fifty miles away. Doc Harmon came here and fixed him up on this very table.' She waved in the direction of the family-sized teapot which sat on a cast-iron trivet.

'On the table!'

'That's right. It's easier that way. Doc deals with everybody in their own homes. Tooth extractions, broken bones, even took out an appendix once when the

Jamieson's little girl took sick.'

Ruby was duly impressed. 'The meal was lovely,' she said at last. 'Cait and I will do the washing-up, by way of thanks.'

'What! After all that travelling! You'll do no such thing! You'll all go up to bed as soon as we're done here, and don't even think about getting up with us in the morning. We'll be up at five to milk, but if you hear us moving about, take no notice. You'll need a day or two to rest up, after coming all the way from the Old Country.'

'You're very kind, but we must get organised soon. Perhaps we'll pop over some afternoon to see these farms they're giving away. I'm sure Danny will be interested.'

Ruby noticed that Jeannie and her grandson exchanged meaningful glances. Had she said something wrong? Perhaps she'd given the impression that they meant to lodge with the Kerrs for some length of time. They must be be careful not to outstay their welcome, particularly when they had come at a difficult time, with Robert Kerr being laid up.

'We'll have a little chat about that tomorrow,' Jeannie said firmly 'Now, up to bed you go, before you fall asleep where you sit. Do you want me to see you up, or can you find your own way?'

The next afternoon, when the Byrne boys were out helping Martin on the farm, Jeannie invited Ruby and Cait into the front parlour. It was well furnished, with two sofas and a rocking chair, a small organ and several small tables, loaded down with knick knacks. Several paintings, executed in sentimental themes, adorned the walls.

'Nice, isn't it?' Jeannie said complacently, seeing Cait glancing about with admiration. 'Some of these things belonged to my husband's parents, and that organ over there came with Beattie, Robert's poor wife. She's dead, of course. We lost her when Martin was a toddler, when she was trying to give birth to twin girls. They outlived her by just three days. I did my best with them, but they weren't meant for this world. Just seven-month babies, they were.'

Ruby nodded. 'It must have been terrible for Mr Kerr.'

'Aye, well, these things happen. But the years have flown by, and here we still are. Now then, Ruby, I need to have a word with you about this farm business.'

'Oh, yes?'

'I don't think you quite realise what you're taking on.'

'I'm sure it's going to be hard work, but I'm used to that.'

'No, you don't understand. I could see that when you mentioned popping over some afternoon. You see, this place you're going to is two thousand miles away. It's more than three days' journey on the train.'

'Two thousand miles!' Cait squeaked. 'Then how on earth shall we get there?'

'Oh, that's not the problem. They have what they call colonist cars, special trains fitted with bunks, and cookstoves. No, it's what you're in for when you get out there that worries me.'

Ruby's face fell. 'I thought it sounded

too good to be true! There aren't any farms going begging, then, are there? It's all a gyp!'

'Oh, it's true enough but I doubt it's what you're expecting. Come on, own up now! What do you see in your mind's eye?'

Ruby thought back to some of the small farms she'd seen in the countryside near Cardiff. White-washed houses, well maintained outbuildings, sheep grazing peacefully in green meadows.

'Aye, you've been expecting something like our place, haven't you?'

'Well, nothing like as grand as this, of course, but . . . '

'Ruby, my dear, what the government is offering your son is a huge tract of land where the soil has never been broken. Nothing more, nothing less. All that will have to be opened up. It will take years to make it prosperous. And settlers have to put up their own houses.'

'What! Then where do they live in the meantime?'

'Tents. Just like the army. And woe

betide them if they don't have a roof over their heads before the snow flies.'

Cait looked at her mother with growing concern.

Ruby seemed to be fumbling for words.

'But surely nobody wants to stay when they find that out, Mrs Kerr?'

'On the contrary, Cait, people are coming out from all over Europe in droves, and they have been doing so for years. Sure, it's hard, but as soon as some of them get settled in, they bring their relatives out to join them. It's a grand future for those willing to work hard.'

'I find this hard to believe,' Ruby said at last. 'Not that I'm doubting your word, mind. But look at your home here, Mrs Kerr.'

'Ah, we're comfortable now, my dear, but when Robert's great grandparents came out from Perthshire this farm was nothing but a hundred acres of forest. They had to cut it all down with axes, before they could even plant a crop.'

'But this lovely house!'

'This house was built forty years ago, when times were prosperous in these parts. Next time you go outside, take a look at the hen house. That was the original log house where the Kerrs lived. It was put up in a day by neighbours, in a house-raising bee. All the farms hereabouts were settled by families from Scotland and Ireland, when times were bad back home and they needed to get out, or starve.'

Cait reached over and patted her mother on the knee. Ruby looked at her miserably.

'I think we've made a mistake in coming here, Cait. Going to the West to farm may be a great opportunity for young men like Danny, and I shan't discourage him from carrying on, but I don't think I'm up to it.'

'What are we going to do, Mam?'

Jeannie Kerr got to her feet. 'Time for a cup of tea, I think,' she murmured. 'I'll put on the kettle, we could do with cheering up.'

'Danny will have to go ahead on his

own,' Ruby decided. 'And perhaps he can take Mickey with him, for all the use the lad will be.'

'You and I, though, we'll have to come up with something else for ourselves. There's always our dressmaking. We might be able to support ourselves with that. Thank goodness we're having the old treadle machine shipped out!'

'Or we could go back to Wales. Just think, we might pass the Singer in the middle of the Atlantic!' They giggled together, but their laughter was tinged with hysteria.

★　★　★

Ruby hadn't expected to get a wink of sleep that night, but in fact she did, and woke up refreshed on their third day in Canada. She found Cait in the kitchen, brewing tea.

'It's all right, I'm not taking liberties. Jeannie told me I could do it.'

'That's all right, then. Where is everybody?'

'She's upstairs, seeing to Mr Kerr, and the boys are out with Martin, taking lessons in how to milk a cow!'

'That should be a sight to behold!'

'Have you thought what we're going to do, Mam?'

'I'm certainly not going out West, and neither should you. Danny can do what he likes, and I shall let him know today. Possibly he can team up with some other young fellow and they can make a go of it together, at least until they get a roof over their heads.'

'But about us,' Cait insisted. 'Shall we go back to Wales? Have we enough money?'

'We might be able to rustle up the fare, but we'd be in dire straits once we landed. Besides, after all we went through, telling people we were off to Canada to make our fortune, I'd hate us to go back with our tails between our legs. No, we'll look for work, try to save a bit, and make a decision then. It shouldn't be too difficult. I'm experienced in shop work, and both of us are good seamstresses. We've come all this way. We should take the chance to see what Canada's all about?'

Cait was pleased to see that her mother had recovered her self confidence and was prepared to put her foot down regarding the ill-conceived notion of going West. And it was true that both of them had skills that would be useful in the new land.

She wondered how Trevor was getting on. Did he ever think of her? She could guess what Mrs Thomas was thinking, now that the Byrnes had gone to Canada; good riddance to bad rubbish! What was the older woman's problem?

Cait sighed. Trevor was Mrs Thomas's one and only lamb. It was natural that she hoped to see him married to someone deserving of him. Yet when it came to social class, there was little difference between Trevor and Cait; both worked as clerks.

Trevor had once mentioned somebody named Ruth, the daughter of his mother's best friend. Apparently the two ladies had had some silly notion of their children growing up to marry each other. No doubt the pair would do their best to throw them together now that Cait was well out of the way.

Why, oh why, hadn't he been able to see Cait's point of view? Was he so much under his mother's thumb that he couldn't think for himself?

How different it would have been if they'd married before the family left for Canada, and Trevor had accompanied them! If he'd wanted to go farming with Danny, she'd have had no hesitation in going West with him, even if it had meant sleeping in the dreaded tent!

Her thoughts were interrupted by the arrival of Martin, who had apparently finished the milking.

'Did you manage to teach Mickey how to do it?' she asked, grinning at the thought.

'Yes and no. Give him his due, the lad did try, but the cow he was working on kicked the pail over, and the milk was lost. Luckily there was only a trickle in it!'

'That's just so typical!'

'Anyway, want to come for a walk?'

'Out to the milking shed, you mean?'

Martin laughed. 'I've done enough teaching for one day, thank you! No, I want to call in at the railway station. I'm expecting a message from my employers to come in by telegraph. I'm anxious to see if it's arrived.'

Cait hesitated. She felt slightly awkward about this. Would it be disloyal to Trevor? She chided herself for being silly. Martin was Danny's pal. He was just being friendly, trying to entertain a guest.

'I'd love to come. I didn't see much of Kildare when we arrived, since it was almost dark.'

'And you won't see much of it now, Cait. We're more than five miles from town here, although the general area is still referred to as Kildare. All we have out here is the station, and even that is known as Kildare Halt. The train stops again in the town proper. Oh, and there's my grandmother's store, of course.'

'Your grandmother has a store? But I thought . . . '

'Oh, Grandma doesn't live at the house. No. After her husband died she bought the store to give herself something to do. She lives in an apartment upstairs. She's only come home for a bit because you're here, and she'll stay on afterwards to give Dad a hand. Normally he manages to feed himself very well, and he's been known to flap a duster around. Of course she does his washing and keeps him supplied with home-baking. Oh, and she bottles a lot of fruit and vegetables in season, and makes pickles galore.'

'She must be a very busy woman.'

Martin shrugged. 'No more so than any farm wife, and she has help in the store. She's the sort of person who likes to keep busy. Better to wear out than rust out, she always says.'

The station agent looked up with a smile as the pair entered.

'There you are, Martin! Good timing. This just came in.' He handed over a form, headed with the address of the railway company. Martin's face broke into a smile, as he pushed the paper into his pocket.

'Thanks, Pete. This way, Cait. We'll have a look round the store.'

He led the way to a two-storey frame building that stood not far from the station. A bell jangled as he pushed open the door.

'Hi, Biddy. Where are ya? Come and meet our visitor, Cait Byrne.'

A woman, heavily pregnant, popped up from behind the counter.

'Gidday, Cait. From the Old Country, aren't ya? I dropped a pile of sugar bags on the floor, and now I can't reach down far enough to pick them up. I meant to weigh out a few pounds while there's nothing doing, but the mail will be in soon, and then I won't have a minute to bless myself with,' The red-haired woman was full of life.

'Here, let me.' Martin retrieved them handily. He turned to Cait. 'As you may have noticed, we have our own Post Office here.' He indicated a tiny cubicle in the back of the room. 'Mail comes in on the train. Some of the old lads from round about will be walking in shortly. Seeing the train come in is the highlight of their day! They'll wait until the mail is sorted, in case there's anything for them.'

'Are we going to wait, too?'

'No, I want to get back, if you don't mind. I've something to do.'

She nodded, taking a last look around the store, which was a veritable Aladdin's cave, holding all kinds of foodstuffs, as well as farm implements, bales of fabric, patent medicines and enough rubber boots to outfit an army.

'Any idea when your gran's coming back?' Biddy asked, as Martin opened the door. 'Only I've a feeling this one won't be long in coming.' She patted her distended stomach cheerfully.

Martin winked at her. 'You can always keep the baby here in a bushel basket, Biddy. Just make sure nobody carries it off instead of potatoes.'

'Oh, you!'

Back at the house, Martin disappeared to find Danny.

Cait took herself into the kitchen, hesitating when she saw a handsome older version of Martin sitting at the table.

'Come ahead in and sit yourself down, girl,' he cried. 'You'll be that young Cait I've heard about, or I'm a monkey's uncle!'

'Hello. Are you Mr Kerr?'

'I was when I got up this morning!'

'How is your arm?'

'Still attached to my body, as far as I can tell, in this plaster.'

Jeannie and Ruby came in then, carrying baskets of vegetables.

'We'll have the first potatoes tonight,' Jeannie said, beaming. 'The shaws haven't died yet, but I thought we could spare a few small ones. There's nothing like new potatoes in parsley butter. Good enough to make a meal in themselves, is what I always say, though tonight I'll be roasting a leg of lamb to go with them.'

Danny burst into the room, with Martin and Mickey at his heels.

'Mam! Mam! You'll never guess what's happened!'

'Steady on, boyo! How about passing the time of day with Mr Kerr first?'

'Sorry, Mr Kerr! How are you feeling?'

'Fair to middling, lad, fair to middling.'

'I've got a job, Mam, working as a bush pilot. What do you think of that, then?'

5

'What do you mean, you've got a job?' Ruby's cheeks had turned pink when she heard what her son had to say. Mickey watched her nervously, well aware from his own experience that this was a sign of trouble to come.

'I'm taking on Martin's job as a bush pilot,' Danny blurted. 'I can't imagine anything I'd like more! But why don't I let him tell it?'

'It's like this,' Martin began. 'Now that Dad's had his accident, I'm needed here on the farm, so I've handed in my notice.'

'You didn't have to do that on my account, son. Mother is here, and we could surely bring in a hired man for the time being.'

Martin shook his head. 'I've had my fill of flying, Dad, and if you must know, I'd rather be on the farm. And Grandma needs to get back to the store soon, with Biddy expecting any day. On the other hand, Dan here is made for the job, and let's face it, he's not cut out for farming. So I wrote to my boss, explaining that I'm needed at home, and recommending Dan to take my place. I couldn't leave them in the lurch, but experienced pilots don't grow on every tree. Mr Cronin's reply came this morning and, as I thought, he's delighted. I'll have to go along on Dan's first trip, to show him the ropes, but then I'll be home for good.'

'Well, I never did!' Jeannie exclaimed. 'Now I'll be able to go back to the store with a clear conscience. Not right away, though,' she added, turning to Ruby. 'It's just that little Mrs O'Connor is so close to her time, and she really shouldn't be on her feet all day.'

'This is a dream come true for me!' Danny was enthused, grinning all over his face from ear to ear. 'I can't wait to get going on this now!'

'What exactly will you be doing?' Cait wondered.

'Ferrying mail and supplies to northern outposts,' Danny told her.

'And goodness knows what else besides,' Martin added. He began a long-winded story about the time he'd had to bring a sick child to the hospital from some isolated spot. Apparently the little boy would have died if this hadn't happened.

'Isn't it wonderful, Mam?' Danny said, his eyes shining.

'Wonderful for some,' she told him, through gritted teeth.

'What's the matter, Mam? Aren't you pleased for me?'

'Oh, yes. Pleased as punch!'

'I don't get it. You seem upset.'

Unnoticed by Ruby, Mr Kerr got up from the table and disappeared into the parlour. Jeannie pushed a bubbling pot to the back of the stove, and followed, closing the door quietly behind her.

'Upset! Why should I be upset? One minute you're going to be a farmer and a wealthy landowner and the next you're flying off into the wide blue yonder. Make up your mind, boyo!'

With his head on one side, Danny's face assumed a puzzled look. 'I have made up my mind. I told you. I'm taking this job. As you keep saying, I know nothing about farming. I am a damn good pilot, though, Mam. If I wasn't, I'd never have come through the war alive. This job is tailor-made for me, don't you see?'

'And what about me, Danny boy? You've talked us all into coming with you to Canada, and now you mean to go off without a thought, leaving us to fend for ourselves. What are we meant to do now, eh? Or do I travel with you, as some sort of baggage handler?'

Cait stifled a giggle at the thought, but Ruby wasn't finished. 'And your brother and sister? What about them? Mickey may have become a farmer in time, but what chance has he got now? The government won't hand out land to a couple of women and a boy!'

'Don't worry, Mam! I've no intention of abandoning you to your fate! I'll get myself established in some sort of base near the aerodrome and then I'll send for you all.'

'Actually we'll be a lot better off this way. We won't have to squander our savings on farm supplies, and I'll be bringing in a good wage. Much better than the pittance I earned in that gents' outfitters back in Cardiff.'

Ruby wasn't convinced. 'And what are we supposed to do while you're off at work for days at time? Sit twirling our thumbs somewhere?'

'Don't make such a fuss, Mam. This is a chance of a lifetime.'

'Now where have I heard that before?' Ruby muttered. Danny laughed, and, clamping a hand on Martin's shoulder, steered him towards the door. There were great matters to discuss. Mickey trailed after them, unsure whether to rejoice or complain.

'What do you think of that, Cait! A bit of a facer, wouldn't you say?'

'I'd say it's all for the best, Mam. You hated the thought of the farm, you know you did. And this way, Danny will be doing work he knows and loves, instead of trying to clear all that land.'

Ruby sighed heavily. 'He's a grown man, and must be free to make his own way. I understand that. I just wish that this job had come up before we left Wales. Then Danny could have come out here on his own, and we could have stayed where we belonged.'

'With no home and no job, you mean!'

'I'm not helpless, my girl. I'd have found some sort of job sooner or later, and as for a home, we could have found temporary digs, I'm sure. And you had a secure job in the Post Office, not to mention a fiance waiting in the wings.'

'That's fallen through, and well you know it.'

'Fiddlesticks. Couples do have these tiffs. It might have sorted itself out eventually. Have you heard from Trevor since we arrived here.'

'No, I haven't.'

'You did give him the Kerr's address, I suppose?'

Cait shook her head.

'Then I suggest you sit down this very day, and write to the boy. At least let him we've arrived safely. No need to get all lovey dovey. Just pen him a cheerful letter, telling him all about the voyage and so on. If he's still interested, he can make the next move. Will you do that, Cait?'

'I might,' Cait said listlessly.

'Meaning you won't! Oh, well, I suppose you're old enough to know your own mind. If it really is all over between you, you could do worse than get together with young Martin Kerr. He seems like a nice lad, and some day he'll inherit this good farm. You could do a lot worse.'

'Mam!'

'All right, all right! I'll say no more.'

Flustered as she was by the change of plan, Ruby found herself drawn into Danny's preparations. It was lucky for him that Martin had done this work before him, because he could offer sensible advice.

'You'd better go down to the store and invest in a couple of flannel shirts and some long johns,' he said. 'Winter will be coming before we know it, and it gets mighty cold in the north, especially when you're flying. You don't want to land on a frozen lake and get frostbitten. And you'll need good leather boots. Rubber's no good in this country.'

'And I'll start on some thick socks for you, lad,' Jeannie promised. 'If our Martin is anything to go by, you'll need as many pairs as you can possibly get.'

'How about you, Ruby? Do you knit? I've a good supply of stocking yarn on order at the store. As soon as it comes in you'd better take your pick before everyone gets wind of it.'

'Oh, Cait and I are both good knitters, though I say it as shouldn't. In fact Cait likes to do Fair Isle jumpers . . . '

'Is that a fact? Perhaps you can make a few, Cait, and we'll sell them in the store. They'd make dandy Christmas gifts, when the time comes.'

'I wouldn't know what size to make them, Mrs Kerr. I couldn't afford to knit garments that might not sell.'

'No problem there! You make one to fit yourself, and we'll have it on display, with a notice saying you'll take orders. And if you do, mind you ask for a deposit each time, or you might get stuck, doing the work for nothing if they don't follow through. Tell people you need to buy the yarn before you can get started. I'd let you have it on tick, of course, but they don't need to know that.'

'Is there a chance that people might refuse to pay for her work?' Ruby said, worried now.

'Oh, people here are honest enough, but a lot of them aren't well off. If the crops fail or some other disaster happens, they have to cut corners. If they've already paid a non-refundable deposit they're more likely to pay the rest and let some other poor soul wait for what's owed them.'

'It sounds all right, but the trouble is, we may not be here much longer. There's no sense doing work to sell here, if we'll be moving on.'

'Well, now,' Jeannie said slowly, 'Robert and I have been having a little talk about that, and we've a proposition to put to you, Ruby. I'll make us a nice cup of tea, shall I, and then I'll round him up and we'll tell you all about it, and see what you think.'

'You'd better hear this as well, Cait,' Jeannie said, as she brought the teapot to the table. 'Come on, Robert, sit yourself down, and let's not keep these folks in suspense.'

'Thank you, Mrs Kerr, if you're sure,' Cait murmured. 'I don't want to butt in if this is something personal.'

'It is, and it isn't, dear. Well, as you already know, one-wing Robbie here needs looking after, and who better to move in and take care of the lad than his own mother? That leaves the store with nobody to keep it open, if Biddy is suddenly taken to her bed. People are used to walking down to the store when they run out of something, and I can just imagine what they'd say if they arrived and found the door locked! They could of course go into town on a Friday night, when the shops stay open until nine for the benefit of the farmers, but that's not the only thing. I'm the postmistress as well, you see.'

'Mmm,' Ruby responded, not quite understanding. Cait, however, had picked up a thing or two from Martin.

'The mail comes in on the train, Mam, and it has to be sorted and put into pigeon holes in the store, for the local people to collect. And the outgoing letters have to be postmarked as well, and put on the train. Isn't that so, Mr Kerr?'

'Aye,' Robert replied. 'Do you know, Mrs Byrne, that if someone wants to contact a friend in town, all Mother has to do is put a letter on the train, and it reaches its destination in fifteen minutes! How's that for efficiency, eh?'

'Remarkable!'

'Some fool down at the lodge the other night reckoned that none of us will be writing letters much longer. Once these new-fangled telephones come in we'll all be talking to each other instead!'

'And with a dozen or more folks on the line, everybody and his dog will be listening in to what's being said!' Jeannie grumbled. 'At least you can seal an envelope and keep your business private. But you're getting me side-tracked, Robert.' She turned to face Ruby.

'So what we were wondering is, how would you like to step in and run the store for me, the pair of you? There's living quarters upstairs, the advantage of that being that when there's no customers you can pop upstairs and cook your meals, or put your feet up. Even if someone does stop by, that bell on the door rings loud enough to wake the dead. Have either of you had any experience in shop work?'

'As it happens, I worked in a green

grocer's before we left Cardiff,' Ruby explained. 'And Cait here was doing well at the Post Office.'

'Better and better! Mind you, we couldn't pay much — not what two people are worth, anyhow — but you'd have your lodging and you'd be able to help yourself to whatever food you fancy from the store.'

'It sounds wonderful, but I really think we ought to start looking for something more permanent. You'll want to return home once Mr Kerr is on the mend, especially when Martin is back to give him a hand.'

'I've been thinking it's about time I retired, Ruby. I'm not as young as I used to be. I might want to let the store go, and move back in here. But that's a long way down the road, and if I did do that we'd have to come to some other arrangement. Now, what do you say?'

'You've not told the woman the whole of it,' Robert interjected, before Ruby had the change to get a word in.

'Oh!' Jeannie hesitated for a moment.

'It's the rural mail, you see. Somebody has to deliver that.'

'I thought Cait said something about pigeon holes. That doesn't sound too difficult.'

'For the past few years we've had rural mail delivery,' Robert said. 'Letters and parcels have to be delivered to the outlying farms. Oh, not door to door. Everyone has a box on a pole at the roadside. The mailman, or mail lady, as the case may be, goes out five mornings a week and leaves the post in those boxes. It's quite simple, really. They're all labelled with the owners' names.'

'And I'd be responsible for that, I suppose. Well, as long as it's not too long a route, I'm used to walking.'

'It's not that simple. The route is close to twenty miles long, and you'll need to go by horse and buggy.'

'What, me?' Ruby let out a squeak which made Jeannie jump.

'Can you not drive a horse, Ruby?'

'I've never tried. I think I might be

afraid of your horse. She seemed quite lively when we came here from the station.'

'Oh, you wouldn't have to take Rascal! No, old Brownie is quite slow and steady, and he knows the route by heart. You wouldn't have any trouble with him.'

'I could give it a try. Unless you'd prefer to have a go, Cait?'

Cait put up both hands, as if to ward off the thought. 'Not me! Ever since I fell off that donkey when you took us to the seaside, I've been terrified of large animals with four legs!'

'Are there any animals who don't have four legs?' Jeannie asked, looking puzzled. 'Never mind, as long as Ruby is willing to give it a go, that's all that matters.'

'And I'll ride with you on your first day, just to give you a bit of confidence,' Robert Kerr promised.

'It seems that all our troubles are over, temporarily at least, thanks to you and your family,' Ruby told Jeannie.

'Think nothing of it, dear. After all, we needed to find someone to help, so it might as well be you.'

'I appreciate it, anyway. All I have to do now is to find a job for young Mickey. I can hardly expect him to go and do it himself. He's just a boy, in a country that's strange to him.'

'Once again, I think we can help you there, Ruby.' Robert Kerr spoke up again. 'I hear they're in need of a boy at the livery stable. As a matter of fact it's the very place where we keep Brownie. It's closer to the store than it is to the farm, which is why we don't stable him here. You'll collect him in the mornings, and check on your boy at the same time.'

'Judging by the ham-fisted way he dealt with Clover the cow, poor Mickey may not do much better with the horses,' Cait remarked, not unkindly, just stating a fact.

Robert laughed. 'I think you'll find he won't have much to do with the animals, Cait. Or at least, not at first.

He's more likely to spend his days mucking out their stalls. It won't do him a bit of harm, though!'

★ ★ ★

The next day found Ruby and her family inspecting their new quarters. Biddy greeted them kindly, pleased to hear that her job was coming to an end.

'My feet are starting to swell,' she confided. 'That's not a very good sign, is it, Mrs Byrne?'

'Oh, you'll be all right if you keep off your feet from now on,' Ruby said tactfully 'You look as though you don't have long to wait now.'

'My due date was last week, Mrs Byrne. I don't know what the hold-up is. My ma says it must be a boy. Boys are always lazy, she says. Do you think that might be true?'

'I suppose it is, sometimes.' Ruby didn't want her son to think that she was putting him down in front of strangers. But Mickey didn't hear what was being said. Instead, he had his hand inside a jar of bull's eyes.

'Cor! This is good, this is! Sweets galore, and all free!'

'Who said anything about free, my lad?'

'That Mrs Kerr said we could help ourselves to what's here. I heard her, honest I did.'

'She said we could feed ourselves from what's in the shop, as part of our pay for running things for her. She didn't say you could eat her out of house and home!' He withdrew his hand, abashed. 'Isn't she paying you any money at all, then, Mam?'

'Not when we're to get free board and lodging, Mickey. However, they'll be giving me a wage for delivering the mail, so I'll be able to save something. Which reminds me, I have to see your new boss, to find out what he'll be paying you. You'll have to stump up part of that to me. Perhaps I should ask him to hand it over to me directly.'

'Aw, Mam!'

106

'Never mind 'aw, Mam!' We don't know how long this state of affairs will last, so we'd be wise to keep something in reserve. If you get on well there you should be able to keep a few pennies in your pocket.'

'Cents, Mam. That's what they call them here. Dollars and cents.' He seemed pleased to be able to air his new knowledge.

Cait smiled. Things were turning out well for them all, after all. The best part was that Mickey was to live at the stable with the other employees, so she would no longer be saddled with the task of trying to get him up in the mornings. Now, if only she knew what was going on with Trevor, she would be much happier.

6

The little train steamed into the station, stopping with a shriek. 'No need to rush out there,' Robert told Ruby. 'The conductor will bring it in. Ewan McPhail, his name is. He sorts the mail on the train and hands us anything that's meant for Kildare Halt. In return, you give him that brown bag there. Biddy's already put the outgoing mail in it.'

Sure enough, the conductor, a tall, thin man, handed Robert a similar bag. With a smile, Ruby handed him the other bag in return, and she was amused when he went red and didn't meet her gaze.

'This is Ruby Byrne,' Robert said. 'She'll be deputy postmistress while my mother is up at the farm, keeping an eye on me.'

'Aye, I heard you took a nasty toss,'

Ewan replied, still avoiding Ruby's glance. 'Bull got you, did it? That's what I heard, any road.'

'Bull my foot! I don't have any such beast. Took a tumble down the ladder from the hay mow, so I did. Nasty enough, mind you. But don't let me keep you, Ewan. The boss man's waving his flag out there, better get going unless you want to run behind the train all the way to Kildare.'

'Very funny, I'm sure. Bye for now, then!'

'He didn't seem to fancy me in the job at all,' Ruby muttered, much to Biddy's amusement.

'You don't want to mind him, Mrs Byrne. He's always been shy around women. That's why he's still a bachelor at his age.'

'I should have mentioned that you're a widow woman,' Robert said.

'Don't give him any ideas! All I want is a quiet life, and if I'm to have that, we should be on our way before the customers put in a complaint!'

Ruby blinked when she saw the conveyance in which she was to deliver the mail. What should it be called, she wondered? A wagon? A trap? Names for so many things were different in this country, and she didn't want to show her ignorance by asking too many questions.

This four-wheeled buggy consisted of a sort of box, in which there was a long seat — big enough for two people, fortunately — and there was an overhead wooden awning that was obviously intended to shield the occupants from the worst of the weather. Brownie, the horse, appeared docile enough, and Ruby felt her fears subsiding.

She put her foot on the step, her hand fluttering to her mouth when the horse moved his front leg, but nothing worse happened and she sank down on the seat, giving a small gasp. Robert Kerr swung himself up with practised ease, only slightly impeded by his broken right arm.

The ride was pure enchantment, as they bowled along in the sunshine. Handling the reins like a veteran, Ruby realised that the horse hardly needed any direction from her. The animal slowed down at each farm lane they came to, only picking up speed again when it appeared that there were no letters to be deposited in the mail boxes.

As she had been told, Ruby saw that the boxes — oblong metal containers — were attached to posts at the roadside. The surname of the customer was painted on the side of each box.

'Do you see those little doo-dads?' Robert asked, pointing to the small hinged flag that was protruding from the first box they came to.

Ruby chuckled at the funny little word. 'Yes. What are they for?'

'If you see one that's been flipped up, you'll know there's outgoing mail in that box. That means you need to stop, even if you have nothing to deliver there. Saves time, you see. You don't need to check every box on the route.'

'Now, when you do have mail to leave, flip the flag up so people know they need to come and fetch what you've left. Most of these farm lanes are a quarter mile long. Nobody wants to hike all the way to the road to find an empty box.'

By the time they reached the end of their route, with Robert chatting away, Ruby found that she knew quite a lot about him. He had been born and brought up on the family farm, and had never been far away from home. As she already knew from Jeannie, his wife had died shortly after the birth of their twin girls, and he had been alone ever since.

'You've never considered remarrying, then?' she asked, regretting the words as soon as she'd spoken. What if he thought she had her eye on him? She'd be mortified! But he didn't seem to find anything amiss.

'I've never met anyone who could take my Beattie's place,' he said. 'What about you, then? Your man died at sea, didn't he? How did that happen? I thought they were all coal miners in Wales.'

'Oh, there's a lot more to Wales than coal mines,' Ruby countered, not really wishing to set him straight, in case he thought she was being smart 'Barney loved the sea, and never wanted to do anything else.'

'It must have been hard on you, though, raising children with your man gone more than half the time.'

Ruby sighed. All of them had looked forward so much to Barney's home-comings. He always had his pockets filled with little gifts for his children, things which had taken his eye in some foreign port. The day when she had finally been forced to accept that he'd never be coming home again was the worst one of her life.

'Oh, well, I managed,' she said at last. 'You do, don't you. No point wishing for the moon.'

Brownie slowed to a halt. Ruby looked up to see a large woman standing at the roadside, her straggly grey hair blowing in the breeze.

'Phew! I didn't think I was gonna make it in time. Can you send this parcel for me, Robert? It's our Maggie's birthday coming up, and I've crocheted her a nice set of dressing table mats. How much is it gonna cost me? Not too much, I hope. The price of everything since the war has gone sky-high.'

'This is Ruby Byrne, Eileen. I'm just showing her the ropes. She's filling in for me while I'm laid up with this arm of mine.'

'Laid up, is it! You don't seem too bad to me, Robert Kerr. Your left arm's still okay, ain't it? Can you not drive with that?'

'Eileen and I were at school together,' Robert explained, observing Ruby's quizzical look.

'That's right! I wore my hair in a braid in them days, and he used to sit behind me and try to dip it in the ink well, the young devil!'

'I did not!'

'You did so!'

'Oh, never mind! Just pass that parcel up here and let us get on with it. Ruby here will leave a note in your box tomorrow, telling how much you owe, and you can leave the money for her to pick up next time.'

On they went, with Ruby enjoying herself so much that she was quite disappointed when they drew up in front of the livery stable. A tall youth stepped forward to help Ruby down before leading Brownie away for a feed and a well-earned rest.

Mickey dashed out of the open door of a box stall.

'Mam!'

'Oh, hello, love. Everything going well, is it?'

He pouted. 'I don't like it here, Mam. I think I'll quit.'

'Oh, no, you don't, my lad! You haven't been here five minutes! What's the matter with the job, anyway? Boss too hard on you, is he?'

'Mr Smith's all right, I suppose. It's

those other fellows. You can't let up for a minute without someone shouting at you to get on. I wish we'd never come to Canada, Mam. It's not fair! Danny gets all the luck. He's flying aeroplanes all over the country and I'm shovelling dung!'

'He's earned his 'luck' as you call it. He went fighting for king and country, taking his life in his hands every time he went up in the air in that contraption. And as for shovelling manure, this job pays far more than you ever earned delivering groceries, and don't you forget it. And if you think you can loll about while Cait and I work to provide for you, you can just think again, because I'm not having it!'

'Byrne!' A red-haired youth hollered at Mickey from across the yard, causing him to run off at a trot. Ruby took a deep breath.

'That boy! He drives me silly at times!'

'I don't suppose it's all his fault,' Robert mused. 'He hasn't had a man in his life to set him straight. Just you leave him here with these youngsters, Ruby. They're all hard-working lads, brought up on the farm. They'll teach him a thing or two.'

'I'm sure I hope so.' Ruby sighed. 'With Danny gone, it's going to be harder than ever for me to manage the child.'

'If I may say so, Ruby, that's where you've been going wrong. Mickey is fifteen. That's practically a man in this country. Time to cut the apron strings and let the lad grow up!'

Ruby clamped her lips together. How dare he lecture her like this? Mickey was her son, and it was up to her to deal with him as she thought best. Still, she was a guest of Robert Kerr's family, and she mustn't fall out with him over such a small thing.

★ ★ ★

'How's it going, Ruby?'

Ruby looked up from her dusting to

find Jeannie at her elbow, with Martin loitering in the doorway. 'Very well, thank you. Cait's a bit worried about doing the butter, though.'

'Oh, she'll soon get the hang of that. Where is she? Upstairs? Up you go, Martin, and give the girl a hand.'

Martin needed no second telling. He found Cait in their small kitchen, staring helplessly at a firkin, a small cask full of butter.

'Give me that mould, and I'll show you what to do,' he ordered. Bemused, she did as she was told. Minutes later she was staring at a pound pat of butter, with a beautiful image of a cow on top.

'You make it look so easy,' she stammered.

'Easy when you know how. When I was growing up, I used to earn my pocket money by doing this for Grandma.'

'Where I come from, you only have to go into a shop and get your butter in a packet.'

'It's the same here, except that we make it up on the spot, and wrap it ourselves. The local farmers bring us their butter, and we give them credit so they can buy other goods in exchange. It's the same with eggs and vegetables, although most people have their own and there's not as much call for them in the store. Farmers sell their extra produce in Kildare. Now then, let's see what you can do with that butter!'

After a couple of false starts, Cait was delighted to turn out several fairly respectable pats of butter.

'Not bad! You're not ready to take any prizes at the county fair, mind you, but it's a good start.'

'How did you know what I was doing?' Cait asked.

'Grandma sent me up. She's here to have a chat with your Ma, about going to the church social.'

'Church social?'

'Yes, we're raising funds for Sunday School supplies. I was wondering if you'd like to go with me, Cait.'

'Er, what happens, exactly?'

'Well, you pay a fee at the door that entitles you to a good supper, and there's dancing afterwards. Everyone comes, even the smallest children. It's a good night out, and you'd get to meet your neighbours.'

'I'm not a very good dancer.' Cait's mind flew back to her days in Cardiff, where she had never been invited to go dancing with Trevor, whose mother thought that the local hops were 'common.' 'I mean, I've heard about the Charleston and the Black Bottom, but I've no idea how you're supposed to do them.'

Martin laughed. 'Neither has anyone else round here. Square dancing and maybe a few reels is what we do in these parts. You'll soon pick them up. No need to be shy, Cait. Do say you'll come! It'll be fun.'

'All right, then, I'd love to. Thank you, Martin.'

She wasn't being disloyal to Trevor, was she? There was nothing between them now. And even if there was, where was the harm? Spending an evening in a crowded church hall, with dozens of other people, was hardly plighting her troth, as the romance novels put it. Although Martin was a very attractive man . . .

She wondered why he didn't have a steady girl friend. Apart from anything else, he was one of those 'daring young men in their flying machines' who had played such a magnificent part in the recent war.

Downstairs, Jeannie and Ruby were discussing the same subject. 'We're having a church supper in a few weeks, in aid of the Sunday School, and I wondered if you'd like to come and work with me and the other ladies? Of course, if you'd rather buy a ticket and come as a supporter, that would be all right, too. This way, though, you'd meet all the other women, and make some new friends while you're at it. There's nothing like working side by side with other folks to get to know them. In any case, they're all eager to meet their new 'postie'!'

'What would I have to do?'

'Part of the work takes place at home, when we bake the pies, and see what sort of pickles we can produce from our store cupboards. That let's you out, but I'm guessing you could manage half a dozen pies?'

Ruby frowned. 'Meat pies, do you mean?'

'No, no. Two layers of pastry, with a fruit filling in between. Surely you have those where you come from?'

Ruby's brow cleared. 'We call those a 'plate of tart' in Wales!'

'What a funny idea! Of course, people also like open pies, such as lemon meringue or pumpkin, but the men seem to prefer raisin, blueberry, cherry or apple.'

'They all sound delicious. I wonder how people manage to choose between all those flavours?'

Jeannie laughed. 'They don't! Most of them take several helpings. That's the beauty of these church suppers. You can eat until you burst, and nobody minds. As I was saying, much of the preparation is done at home. We make baked beans, and bowls of salad, and peel potatoes to be cooked in the church kitchen on the day. Somebody else cooks the hams, and there you are! I know it sounds like a lot, but most of it can be done sitting down, in our own homes.'

'I'm sure I could do all that,' Ruby said bravely. After all, if a group of elderly ladies were willing to do it, she could hardly fail to keep up with them at the relatively youthful age of forty-five!

'I feel bound to tell you that there is a downside to all this,' Jeannie went on, 'and that's all the washing up! Still, we do that to music, and many hands make light work, as the saying goes. There's just a counter between the kitchen and the main hall, so after they've eaten we can watch the dancing as we work. The sound of the fiddles drowns out any clatter we might make.'

'I'm sure Cait would be willing to help, too,' Ruby said.

'Ah! Well that's another thing. Our Martin means to invite her to go with him. He'll introduce her to all his friends, and she'll have a high old time. He'll be up there asking her at this very minute, I'm sure.'

'He can ask, but I'm not sure of her reaction, Jeannie.'

'Got a young man back home, has she?'

'Yes and no. I'm not sure where we stand now. She was walking out with this boy; Trevor, his name is. But he was very much under his mother's thumb and, reading between the lines, I suspect that it was this Mrs Thomas who prevented him from making the commitment our Cait was looking for. When Danny persuaded me to come out here with him, bringing Mickey as well, of course, Cait insisted she meant to stay behind. Then, at the last minute, she changed her mind. I gather that

Trevor's reaction wasn't all she'd hoped for.'

'It sounds like one of those romance books they have in the Kildare library. Did she hope it would ginger him up a bit, telling him she was leaving for Canada?'

'Now that I can't say. If she did plan on that, it failed miserably, because obviously she's here, and he's back there!'

'Then there's nothing to prevent her accepting Martin's invitation, is there? And if she's too shy to go as a guest, just you bring her along to join the Willing Workers. That's what we call ourselves, you know. I don't know who thought that one up — a bit before my time, I'd say — but it describes us to a tee.'

'Your church ladies certainly sound enthusiastic,' Ruby remarked, overwhelmed at the thought of all that pie-baking.

'We're having a quilting bee next week, too, finishing up a quilt to be raffled off in aid of the missions. You've told me you're both good with a needle, so there's no excuse for you to miss that. We stitch away and have a good gossip at the same time. You'll learn more about this neighbourhood in an hour around the quilting frame, than you would in a month, working here at the store.'

Jeannie opened the door at the foot of the stairs, and bellowed up loudly, as though she was calling the cows home.

'Come on, Martin! Let's go, unless you plan to stay up there all day!'

'I'm on my way, Grandma!'

Ruby went back to her dusting. Things were looking up. She not only had an interesting job, but she was on the verge of making new friends. And if Cait was still fretting over Trevor, it would be good for her to get out and about. Danny had the job of his dreams, and he had promised faithfully that he would write to her from time to time, telling her all about his exploits. She longed for the day when, sorting the mail, she would come across an envelope addressed in his sprawling handwriting.

Mickey, too, was settled, or at least, Ruby hoped that he was. If he comes sauntering through that door, claiming to have left his job, he'll be in trouble, she vowed. It was time he learned responsibility!

7

'This is Miss Byrne, who has come to speak to us today. Can you say good morning to her?'

'Good morning, Miss Byrne,' the children chorused, in a sing-song fashion.

Cait glanced around the room, which contained several rows of two-person desks, clustered on either side of a wood-burning stove. The day was too warm for it to be in use today, but she could well imagine how necessary it would be during the winter months. Miriam Crockett, standing very upright on the low platform that supported her desk, waved her pointer in the air.

'Miss Byrne has come all the way from Wales. That is a place in England. Who can find England for us on the map?' She pointed to a small, pig-tailed girl who bustled importantly to the front of the room. The child pointed to

Britain, and was rewarded with an approving smile.

Cait found herself in a dilemma. Miriam wasn't the first person she'd met to have made that mistake. An elderly woman, the one person who actually did know something about Wales, had asked her if she 'spoke Garlic' and it had been all she could do to respond sensibly, when she really wanted to say 'no, and I don't eat it, either.' The poor old soul was only trying to be friendly.

Similarly, it would have been quite wrong to correct the teacher in front of her pupils, but all Cait's Welsh ancestors rose up in protest now, at least in the back of her mind! She produced the flag she had drawn, took a deep breath, and sailed into her presentation.

'Can anyone tell me what this is?' she asked.

Hands shot up. 'It's a flag, Miss.'

'Very good. It is the flag of Wales, where I come from. Wales is a country which has its own language, its own national anthem, and of course its own flag . . . '

A small boy waved his hand vigorously to get her attention.

'Yes?'

'I think that's the flag of China, Miss. It's got a dragon on it, see.'

'I'm afraid not. That's the red dragon of Wales. I'll tell you a story about that, if you'd like to hear it.'

There were nods all round.

'Once upon a time, there was a boy called Merlin . . . '

After that she had their interest, and the rest of the lesson passed quickly, while the questions came thick and fast.

When at last the ordeal was over, Miriam stepped forward, baring her teeth in what Cait thought was an insincere smile.

'I'm sure we all enjoyed that, didn't we, children? How about a round of applause for Miss Byrne, for coming to tell us all about England?'

Hearty clapping followed, which escalated into cheers when the pupils were told they could go outside for recess. Cait turned round to witness Miriam in the act of clasping Martin by the arm.

'Thanks so much for stopping by, Martin!'

Hey, what did he do? Cait wanted to say, but she held her tongue.

'You'll be coming to the church social, won't you? Do you want to come in and pick me up? We can walk over together.'

'Sorry, Miriam, but I'm already taking Cait, here.' Martin spoke easily, but Cait hardly knew where to look. Miriam somehow managed to look cross and disappointed at the same time.

'Oh, well then, another time, perhaps. Actually John Beeton invited me, but I told him I might be going with you.'

'You shouldn't count your chickens, then, should you!' Martin grinned cheerfully to take the sting out of the words.

Miriam pouted. 'We've always gone together before.'

'We did last year, but only because somebody who couldn't go at the last minute made you a present of the two tickets.'

Cait hid a smirk. That trick was as old as the hills.

The agony aunts in women's magazines were always advising lovelorn girls to pretend they'd been given tickets for some outing, and use this as an excuse to ask a man out. It was silly, really. Why should a woman have to wait for a man to issue an invitation? Far simpler to approach him instead. But that was the custom, and so far society hadn't found a way to change it.

'Perhaps you should go with Miriam,' she ventured, as they walked back up the road, within earshot of the joyful shrieks of children at play. 'I don't mind at all. I can go with Mam and help with the other ladies.'

'Why would I want to do that? I'm looking forward to taking you. I've known Miriam forever, Cait. As I mentioned earlier, we were at school together. We're like brother and sister.'

Men! Martin must be blind if he thought that! Anyone could see that the girl was determined to get her hooks into him.

'I'll admit we did go out together once or twice — when we were fifteen! Apart from that, the two of us were just part of the crowd. When we were growing up a bunch of us used to do things together. Skating on the pond in winter, going on hay rides in the fall. That sort of thing. There was never anything to it, unless you count an inept kiss when we were playing spin the bottle!'

'People grow up, and feelings change.'

'Not in our case. Miriam put up a great fuss when I went away to war, and at first I thought she was upset in case something happened to me. But I asked her to keep in touch, and I didn't receive a single letter. That's Miriam for you. Always blowing hot and blowing cold.'

Cait wasn't convinced. Seemingly Martin knew his own mind and he had no interest in Miriam, other than a long-standing friendship. But when it came to Miriam it was a different matter, and this was made evident when the young school teacher came into the store later.

'Can I help you?' Ruby stepped forward, all smiles.

'Oh, I thought that Miss Byrne was in charge here.'

'You know Cait, do you?'

'If that's her name. I teach at the school. She came to speak to the children the other day.'

'Of course. Just a minute. I'll call her down.'

'Hello, Miss Crockett.' Cait wondered what she wanted.

'Miss Byrne. I wondered if you had a bay leaf.'

'A bay leaf?' Ruby looked up at the shelf, where tins of parsley, sage and pepper stood in neat rows. 'I don't think we do. There doesn't seem to be much call for things like that. I'm afraid you'll have to try one of the larger shops in town.'

'Would there be anything else?' Cait asked, putting on a false smile. Why on earth had she been brought all the way downstairs, when Mam was quite capable of serving in the shop? Miriam must want to get a message across.

'No. This is really too bad. I did think you might have a bay leaf. Now I'll have to hitch up the horse and go all the way to Kildare.'

'What did you want it for? I could suggest a substitute,' Ruby said.

'I'm trying out a recipe for boeuf bourguignon. It calls for a bay leaf.'

'That's only a fancy name for beef stew,' Ruby told her. 'I'm sure you can manage without the bay leaf.'

'But I'm entertaining a very special guest tomorrow evening.'

'Your young man, is it?'

Miriam simpered. 'Yes, if you like to put it that way. Perhaps you know him.

Martin Kerr, whose grandmother owns this store.'

Cait and Ruby exchanged looks. Jeannie had invited them both to the farm for supper the following evening, and Ruby knew for a fact that Martin would be present. Cait had explained that he had asked her to be there early, so they could take a walk before the meal. He wanted to show her his favourite spot, down by the river, where he had played as boy. And he had no plan to leave as soon as supper was over, for he'd mentioned playing games in the parlour, crokinole and Chinese chequers, neither of which Cait had heard of before. There was no suggestion of Martin slipping away to join Miriam!

Now Miriam shot a triumphant glare at Cait, who looked down at her feet while counting to ten. Battle had been joined!

'Don't mind her,' Ruby counselled, when Miriam had sailed out of the shop, without bothering to latch the door behind her. 'Sour grapes, that's all it is. I reckon she's a real dog in the manger. She didn't want him until you came on the scene, and now she's determined to get him into her clutches.'

'That's what I'm afraid of,' Cait said.

8

The door bell pinged and Ruby looked up. The train had just steamed in, and she was expecting to see the conductor, Ewan McPhail, bringing in the mail. Instead it was two men from the section gang, fellows whose job it was to keep the tracks cleared.

'Morning, Missus! How are you this fine day?'

'Good morning. If you've come about that chewing tobacco, I'm expecting it to come in on the train today. Does the baggageman have any packages for me this morning, I wonder?'

'He said he'll be here in a minute. Mind if we wait? It helps the work along if a fella's got something to chaw on.'

'Please yourself,' Ruby said, continuing to assemble the outgoing mail. The door pinged again. This time it was Ewan. They exchanged bags as usual, but he stood in front of her, shuffling his feet.

'Yes? Is there something I can help you with?'

'Er, I was thinking . . . ' he hesitated for moment.

'Yes? What is it?'

He cast a helpless look at the grinning section men and left.

'Now what was all that about?' Ruby wondered aloud at his actions.

'Guess he's sweet on you, Missus.'

'Don't talk nonsense!' Flustered, Ruby was thankful when the baggage man came in, staggering under the weight of two large cardboard boxes.

'Give us a hand, will you?' he croaked, and the larger of the two section men lumbered forward to do as he asked. Later, Ruby mentioned the encounter to her daughter.

'What fun!' Cait remarked, her eyes twinkling. 'Imagine having two men after you, Mam!'

'What on earth are you talking about?'

'Why, first Robert Kerr, and now

Ewan McPhail. Which one will you end up with, I wonder?'

'Now you're being silly. Robert is a good friend, that's all. Once his arm is better, and he starts delivering the mail again, that's the last I'll see of him, I daresay.'

'Never mind, you'll have Ewan now.'

'Cait. Stop that, will you? Such foolish talk. Anyway, I have no idea what he was about to say. He never did get it out. He may have been wanting to buy something but was too shy to ask in front of the others.'

'Like what, for instance?'

'I don't know. Underwear, perhaps.'

Cait raised her eyes to the ceiling. 'Why should he be embarrassed about that? We sell men's clothing every day of the week, don't we? Well, Mam, as I see it, you've got two choices.'

'Such as?'

'Either forget about it, or ask him what he was going to say.'

'I'm sure I don't know why we're having this conversation,' Ruby snapped. 'I simply made an off-hand remark, and you've turned it into some kind of inquisition. If you've nothing better to do with your time, I suggest you go and get on with cleaning the parlour. It's your turn this week, and well you know it! And while you're at it, these front windows could do with a wipe over.'

'Yes, Mam, I'll see to it. You want to be able to spot these beaux of yours when they come calling!'

Ruby had to wait a week before she learned just what Ewan McPhail had in mind. He came into the store, cap in hand, and took up his position at the end of the counter, so that she was trapped behind it.

'Yes, Mr McPhail. Can I get you something?'

'It's about the church social,' he blurted. 'Would you do me the honour . . . That is . . . Will you come with me? I'll pay for the ticket.'

Ruby took deep breath. 'It's kind of you to ask me, Mr McPhail, and I'm very flattered, but I'm afraid I'm already committed.'

'I suppose it's Robert Kerr, isn't it.'

'No, it's not. I've agreed to work at the supper, with the other ladies.'

'Surely you can say you've changed your mind?'

'I'm afraid not. I've given my word, and I won't break it now.'

'I understand,' he said, looking crest-fallen, 'but I don't give up that easily. I'll come up with something else we can do, and we'll see what you say to that. Good morning, Mrs Byrne.'

'Er, good morning, Mr McPhail.'

'Now what am I going to do?' Ruby demanded, when Cait emerged from behind the store room door, her eyes sparkling. 'I don't know the man from Adam. I don't know that I should agree to go out with him. What if he gets serious and proposes marriage or something, and I can't manage to wriggle out of it? He's seems like a decent chap, and I don't want to hurt him.'

'Aren't you jumping the gun a little, Mam? It's a big jump from the church supper to a marriage proposal.'

But Ruby wasn't so sure. She didn't quite know how things were done in these parts, but she was fairly sure that turning up on a man's arm at some church event was tantamount to some sort of declaration of intent. At the very least every eye would have been upon them, and they would have been the subject of whispered gossip for weeks. It was just as well that she'd had a good reason for turning the man down.

When Ewan ventured in a week later, looking much more confident now, she could think of no valid excuse. 'I thought you'd like a ride on the train,' he announced. 'You haven't been on it before, have you?'

'We did come on it when we first arrived.'

'I heard about that, and I guess you didn't see much then, it being nearly dark. You want to see something of the countryside now. It's pretty at this time of year, with all the goldenrod in bloom.'

'I've bought your ticket, and I'll

collect you tomorrow morning.'

'Er, I don't know that I should leave the store unattended.'

'That girl of yours will be here. She's more than capable of looking after things for a while?'

'But I'm the mail courier. You know that, don't you?'

Ruby was running out of excuses now.

'Tomorrow is Saturday,' he said firmly. 'You don't deliver mail then.'

'We're going on the up-train to the end of the line, and then we'll come home on the down-train.'

'Should I bring sandwiches?' Ruby asked, bowing to the inevitable.

'No, no. We can get a bite to eat at the other end.'

So, early the next morning, Ruby set off, for her date with destiny and returned on the evening train, weary and ready for a strong cup of tea.

'How did it go, Mam? Did you have a good time?'

Ruby groaned. 'That beastly train

stopped at every little flag stop along the way. And you'll never guess what happened! All of a sudden one of the other passengers let out a squawk, saying he'd seen a puffball, growing in a field near the tracks. They only stopped the train, Cait, and Mr McPhail climbed out and went and brought it back. 'Anyone want a steak?' he shouted, and then he cut the thing into slices and handed them round. Apparently that sort of thing happens quite often. A woman sitting next to me said that one day back in the spring everyone trooped off the train so they could pick wild strawberries in a nearby field. Did you ever hear the like? Only in Canada!'

She reached up to pull the hat pin out of her straw boater.

'A woman sitting beside you? Mr McPhail didn't sit with you, then?'

'Certainly not! He was working, if you can believe that! I went all that way, just to watch him striding up and down, collecting tickets.'

'I gather you won't be seeing him again, then.'

'That I won't. Honestly, Cait, I can quite see why he's remained a bachelor until now. What woman would have him?'

9

'You know, I believe it's time we threw a dinner party,' Ruby remarked to Cait, stopping to lick her indelible pencil as she made a list on the back of a sugar bag.

'Who were you thinking of inviting, then? I suppose it's only right that you return Mr McPhail's hospitality. He gave you such a wonderful outing to the back of beyond.'

'No, you fool! The Kerrs have been so good to us ever since we arrived. The very roof over our heads is a result of their good nature. I mean to ask Jeannie and Robert, and naturally I can't leave Martin out. I take it you have no objection to sitting at the table with him?'

'No, of course not. Why should I? And take a look in the mirror, Mam. Your tongue's gone all purple from licking that pencil.'

Ruby tutted at the sight. 'Mickey has been given Sunday off, so I thought that would be a good day to entertain. What do you think?'

'Mmm. What about food?'

'I thought a loin of pork, with trimmings, and a treacle tart to finish.'

'Mickey's favourite.'

'That's right. I hope the Kerrs will like it. Robert has something of a sweet tooth, I understand.'

'Why wouldn't they like it?'

'Oh, it's just that it doesn't seem to be known here. I was going to make half a dozen to take to the church supper, but now I'm not so sure. It would be too bad if I used up all those ingredients only to have the tarts go to waste. That's why I'm testing them out on the Kerr men.'

When Sunday arrived, Mickey duly came home, sniffing the air like a cat scenting a lurking mouse.

'Something smells good. Is there any treacle tart?'

Ruby surveyed her son fondly. 'Hello,

Mam! How are you, Mam? Good to see you. There is tart, yes, but that's for later. I did make a few jam tarts with the leftover pastry, though. You can have one of those.'

'Thanks,' he mumbled, pushing one into his greedy mouth.

'My goodness! Don't they feed you at that place? And I've told you before, don't smack your mouth when you're eating.'

'It's hours since breakfast. Can I have a sandwich, to tide me over?'

'You'll have a bath before you do anything else, my lad. I'm not having you come to the table smelling of horse.'

Grumbling, he went to do as he was told. Later, when the Byrnes and their guests had said grace, and Ruby had started to dish up, she noticed that the boy seemed to be in deep consultation with Robert. What on earth could that be about? She was soon to find out.

'Mam, I've something to tell you. I've given in my notice at the livery stable,' he remarked.

Ruby's heart sank. Here we go again, she thought. He was up to his old tricks, and he'd chosen this moment to let her know, because she could hardly throw a fit in front of company

'Then you'll just have to go and take it back,' she told him, making a valiant attempt to keep her voice even. 'You mustn't keep chopping and changing, or you'll get a bad reputation. And you need to work. We all do. It's vitally important for each of us to toe the line when we've just come to a new country.'

'Let me finish, Mam. I'm going to the lumber camp for the winter.'

'The what?'

Robert leaned across the table. 'Perhaps I can explain, Ruby. Each winter, when things are quiet on the farm, and the women and children can be left to manage on their own, many men go to cut timber. It's a grand way to earn extra money. In a few weeks you'll see them all going north on the train. Each camp has its own large shanty, where the men live when they're not working. In the spring the logs are floated down the river, and that's how they bring them out of the bush, to market.'

'Oh, no you don't, Michael Byrne!' His mother was absolutely horrified. 'Isn't it bad enough to have one son flying in the wilderness, without sending another one into terrible danger? And I've read about these river drivers! They balance themselves on all those floating logs, manoeuvering them with some sort of long poles. And what do they get for their pains?' Tears poured from Ruby's eyes.

'Mickey wouldn't be doing any such thing, Ruby!' Robert patted her hand. 'He's going as a chore boy. Carrying hay and water to the horses, who are taken there to skid the logs out from the bush to the riverbank. Carrying water for the cook. That sort of thing. I did it myself.'

It suddenly occurred to Ruby that Robert seemed to know altogether too much about Mickey's plans.

'You arranged this, didn't you!' she accused him.

'As it happens, I did. The boy heard the other lads talking about it, and he decided he'd like to give it a go. We thought you'd be pleased. Once he's in camp he'll be there until spring. There'll be no giving up and quitting that job, no matter how hard he finds it.'

'I should have been consulted first!'

There was silence around the table. Jeannie looked uncomfortable, and Cait hoped that her mother would manage to control her temper, at least until their guests had gone. She was just about to get up to clear away the plates when Mickey, no doubt feeling that he should change the subject to smooth things over, spoke up. Being Mickey, he managed to put his foot in it.

'Are you going to marry that man, Mam?'

'What man, for goodness' sake?' Bewildered, Ruby glanced at Robert, and then at Cait.

'That fellow who works on the train. Evans or something. One of the fellows I work with has a brother on the section gang. He says that conductor is sweet on you.'

'Oh, that. It's nothing. It's just a joke at my expense, I expect. Those cheeky section men often drop in here to buy their baccy, and they see Mr McPhail coming in with the mail bags and think it's funny to make silly remarks. Of course there's nothing going on.'

But despite Ruby's warning glares, and the sharp kick delivered under the table by Cait, Mickey didn't know when to leave well alone.

'But you have gone out with him,' he persisted.

'If you must know, I had a ride on the train one Saturday. There was no more to it than that. He thought I'd enjoy seeing the countryside, although he was working at the time. So I went along with it. Is there anything wrong with that?'

'Just so long as you know they're all

talking about you, Mam.'

Sensing Ruby's embarrassment, Jeannie murmured about the weather having been good for the crops, and Martin chimed in at once, talking about the selling price for cattle.

Cait stole a look at Robert, who had gone quiet. Mickey seemed to have set the cat among the pigeons in a big way. 'How about a game of euchre?' she enquired, knowing that the Kerrs enjoyed a card game.

The evening dragged on interminably, until Mickey finally stood up and said that he had to be getting back. On cue, Jeannie also pushed back her chair.

'This was lovely, Ruby. Thank you so much. And you will let me have the recipe for that tart, won't you? A little sweet for my taste, perhaps, but the boys loved it.'

'I'm glad they enjoyed it. We must do this again sometime.'

'But not if Mickey's around,' Cait muttered, sotto voce.

Jeannie waited while Ruby went to

copy out the recipe, and Martin followed Cait downstairs, saying something about an outing to the picture palace in Kildare. The coming film, *One Week*, starring Buster Keaton, and was supposed to be quite good.

As the pair of them lingered at the door, Cait could see Robert Kerr, stumping away down the road in the direction of the farm. What he'd heard obviously hadn't pleased him at all! The question was, would this provoke him into proposing something to Ruby? Or had he been turned off by the knowledge that she'd been seeing somebody else, as well as himself? Only time would tell.

★ ★ ★

Three days went past, and still Robert did not put in an appearance. Jeannie dropped in, to say thank you for the lovely evening, and once or twice Martin popped in when he happened to be passing by.

'Drat that Mickey!' Ruby muttered, when she realised that Robert was avoiding her. 'Why did he have to go and open his mouth like that? None of his business, in any case, although it was most unfortunate that those railroad men are such gossips.' She said as much to Cait.

'My mother, the femme fatale,' Cait said, laughing.

'Now don't you start! I'm a perfectly respectable, middle-aged widow. I don't like it when people take my name in vain, and I particularly don't care for it when Robert Kerr takes umbrage because I took a perfectly innocent train ride, without asking his permission.'

'I expect he's hurt; don't you think?'

'He's no reason to be! It's not as if there was anything between us. Robert and me, I mean.'

'Do you suppose he sees it like that, though?'

'What are you trying to say, Cait?'

'Well, you have been seeing a lot of each other. He may have read more into the relationship than there actually was, especially when you invited him over for a meal.'

'I didn't invite him for a meal, as you put it. The whole family came, and you know why that was. Merely a little acknowledgement of everything the Kerrs have done for us. And now I come to think of it, that hasn't been all one-sided. Yes, we have jobs and a roof over our heads, but we're helping them out in their time of need. Not that I expect gratitude, but this is a two-way street.'

'I expect it will all come out in the wash.' Cait sighed, but she wasn't really concerned. If Robert Kerr wanted to sulk, that was his problem.

The more she thought about it, the more annoyed Ruby became. She had a bone to pick with Robert over this business of Mickey spending the winter in the lumber camp. These arrangements simply should not have been made behind her back.

Any mother worth her salt would have wanted a say in the matter. What if the boy became ill, and there was no way for her to reach him? Anything could go wrong. Mickey could be a terrible nuisance at times, but he was her son, and she loved him. She wouldn't have a moment's peace until he came safely home in the spring. Perhaps there was still time to nip this business in the bud?

One morning, while organising the outgoing mail, Ruby glanced out of the window, alerted by the shriek of the approaching train. Her heart leapt when she saw Robert standing outside. Where could he be going at this time of day? Surely he wasn't waiting to see Ewan McPhail? She had visions of poor Ewan with blood streaming down his smart navy-blue uniform, after being hit on the nose by his rival.

But that was a foolish thought. Quite apart from anything else, Robert was in no condition to deliver a punch, not when his arm was in plaster. The train arrived, Robert mounted the steps, and was lost from view.

When Martin called in later that

morning, carrying a letter to post to a pal in England, someone he'd met while serving in the Flying Corps, Ruby found she could stand it no longer.

'Where was your dad off to this morning? I saw him get on the train.'

'Oh, he's only gone to see Doc Harmon.'

Ruby's heart gave an unwelcome flutter. 'He's not ill, is he?'

'Of course not. The Doc would come out to see him if he was. No, if his arm seems to be all right he'll be getting the plaster sawn off today. He'll probably have to do a few exercises to get it back into shape but he should be able to take back his mail route soon. I expect you'll be glad to get shot of it before winter comes. Once the snow starts we'll take the wheels off the buggy and replace them with runners, and that's a whole different ball game, driving in the snow.'

Ruby felt sad to think of giving up her daily excursions to deliver the mail. She'd enjoyed the freedom of travelling the countryside, apart from those occasions when the heavens had opened and she'd come home drenched. She'd enjoyed chatting to the various customers who met her at the roadside, and she'd gladly undertaken their small commissions, bringing items from the store, or delivering something to a neighbour who lived farther down the line. All that would soon be over.

Of greater concern was the thought that Jeannie might no longer be needed at the farm and would want to return home. Ruby had come to love the cosy little apartment over the store, and she knew that Cait was happy too. Where would they go, if they received their marching orders?

When the evening train arrived, she searched anxiously to see if Robert was getting off. Somehow she missed seeing him, so it was a shock when she turned away from the counter, reaching for a package of tea demanded by a customer, and saw him standing at the back of the line. When his turn came she tried not to meet his eye.

'Is there something you want, Robert?'

'Are you going to lock up now? All right, go ahead. Then perhaps you'll invite me upstairs and brew up. That train took forever to get here, and I'm parched.'

Silently, Ruby did as he asked, before marching upstairs.

'Now, then. Do you have something you have to say to me?'

'Put the kettle on first, why don't you. Is Cait here?'

'I believe she's reading in her bedroom. Why do you want to know?'

'Must you ask so many questions, woman? What I need to know is what you think of me.'

Ruby was taken aback by this. Stalling for time, she made the tea and brought everything to the table, slowly placing cups on saucers, and adding teaspoons. 'Well, are you going to answer me or not?'

'I'm not sure what you mean, Robert.'

'I'm asking you, am I the sort of man you'd be willing to marry?'

She gasped. Whatever she'd been expecting, it certainly wasn't this!

'I believe you're a good man, Robert. I'm sure any woman would be glad to marry you.'

'That's not quite what I meant. If I were to ask you right now, would you agree to be my wife?'

'But you're not asking me, are you? So the question is academic.'

'Oh, for goodness sake!' He jumped up and took her in his arms. When she'd begun to recover from his ardent kiss, it was to see Cait standing in the doorway of her room, with her hand covering her mouth.

'What are you looking at, my girl?'

'Sorry, Mam. I was just . . . '

Robert swung around to face the astonished girl. 'I was just asking your mother if I could become your step-father,' he explained, with a huge grin all over his face.

'My step . . . ' Cait turned and fled.

'Is she very upset, do you think?' Robert was looking anxious now.

'Come to think of it, what about you? I hope I haven't been too forward. I do want to marry you, Ruby. What is your answer going to be?'

'I don't mean to sound like a Victorian heroine, Robert, but this is a bit sudden and I'll need time to think. I thought you were fed up with me because of what Mickey said.'

'I was upset to hear you'd been out on a date with Ewan McPhail!'

'I'm sure I don't know why. I'm a free agent, after all.'

'But we've been going out together for weeks!'

'As friends, yes, but we didn't have any sort of understanding.'

'But you see, I thought that we did. I haven't looked at another woman since my Beattie died. It seems as though my heart has been frozen all these years. Then, when I met you, I couldn't believe how my feelings came alive again.'

'I don't know as I feel just the same as I did back then, when I was young and impressionable, but I guess it's what a person might call a mature love. I'll make you a good husband, Ruby, and I can offer you a good home, and your Cait, as well. Of course, if things go as our Martin is hoping, she may be coming into the house by right.'

'Ah, now that's another thing. I'm not sure what may be going on there, but I'm very much afraid that her heart is already well and truly spoken for. I do hope that your Martin isn't going to be hurt.'

'He's mentioned some Welsh chap, but he seems to be under the impression that he's out of the picture now.'

'Don't count on it, Robert. I'm afraid I've taken it upon myself to do something that we may all live to regret. Still, time will tell.'

'Martin and Cait will have to work things out for themselves. Right now, I'm only concerned with you and me. Can you give me answer now, Ruby girl?'

Ruby sat up straighter in her chair and looked at him tenderly. 'Yes, Robert Kerr, I'll marry you,' she told him.

10

On the night before the wedding, Ruby and Cait sat up talking into the wee hours. It was as if they needed to put the past behind them, to draw a line beneath their old lives and what was yet to come.

Danny and Mickey had come back from their jobs for the grand occasion, and even now they were sleeping in Cait's room, while she was sharing a bed with her mother.

'I'll never forget your father,' Ruby said softly. 'He was the love of my life, but he's gone, and nothing can ever bring him back. I like to think that if he can look down and see me now, he approves of what I'm about to do. Robert is a good man and I'll be safe with him.'

'I suppose you two have that in common, Mam. Robert lost his wife when she was very young. Martin took me to the graveyard to see where his mother and little sisters are buried.'

The girls had a beautiful little tombstone with two hearts carved on it. One heart commemorated Janet Kerr, aged three days, and the other was dedicated to Marion Kerr, aged two days. A nearby stone was that of Beattie Grant, aged twenty four years, beloved wife of Robert Kerr.

'I've seen it too, Cait, and wept a tear or two over it. So much sadness, and so long ago. At least Robert had a place to visit and grieve.' She was silent for a moment, remembering her Barney in his watery grave.

'Never mind, Mam. The two of you have years of happiness ahead. You have so much to look forward to.'

'God willing,' Ruby said. She had learned long ago that it didn't do to take life for granted. One never knew what might lie just around the corner. Better to live in the moment and let tomorrow take care of itself, if only you could.

Once she and Robert had returned from their honeymoon, they would be living at the farm together, along with Martin. Jeannie had expressed her intention of going back to her beloved store, although she had promised her son that she would try to slow down a bit. She was getting on a bit, and on damp mornings, when she struggled to get out of bed, she certainly felt her age.

'I'm creaking like an old barn door,' she liked to say.

She had invited Cait to stay on with her, getting a wage for working in the store. 'As you know, we have the two bedrooms, so you can keep the one you've been using.'

Ruby wondered how this would work out. Jeannie was a lovely person, but quite set in her ways and used to having employees who did as they were told.

'It won't be the same as working alongside me,' she warned.

'I know, Mam, but I mean to give it a go. If it doesn't work out I can always go back to clerical work. I know there's nothing like that here, but if necessary I can move into town and take a room somewhere. After working in the Post Office in Cardiff I'm well trained in all the ins and outs of that work. I should be able to land a job quite easily.'

Ruby bit her lip. 'What about you and Martin? Is there any hope of a bit of romance there?'

Cait shook her head. 'I have a feeling that he'd like there to be, but no, Mam. At one time I did wonder if our friendship could develop into something more, but no. I can safely say that there's nothing like that on my side. In fact, I've been giving him subtle hints in that direction. I'd hate to have him propose to me, only to be turned down. He's a lovely man, and I wouldn't hurt him for the world. Besides, it would only make things awkward for you, if Martin and I had a falling out. You have to live under the same roof with him, after all.'

'Just think, I'll be his stepmother,' Ruby marvelled. 'But I must ask you this. Are you still in love with Trevor Thomas?'

Cait lowered her head, saying nothing. It was obvious that she still had deep feelings for the man.

'Then I have a confession to make, lovey.'

'What have you done, Mam?'

'Some time ago I wrote to Trevor, giving him our address.'

'You didn't!'

'I'm afraid I did. Just a newsy letter, telling him what we were all doing. I thought he deserved to know how to get in touch with you, Cait. It wasn't kind of you to cut him off so completely, even if he was dithering a bit when you tried to pin him down.'

'Oh, Mam!'

'And have you heard anything in return?' Ruby knew very well that no letter had come with a Cardiff postmark. After all, she was the one who sorted the incoming mail.

Cait shook her head sadly. Ruby took a deep breath and sailed in.

'Then it's probably all for the best, dear. I know it hurts now, but this will help you to make a clean break, once and for all. Who knows, in time you may come to care for Martin after all. First love is painful, but there's something to be said for a more mature love, based on trust and companionship, such as I've found with Robert.'

'No, Mam. I'll never marry. I shan't mind a bit being single. It will give me the chance to experience everything Canada has to offer. When I've saved a bit of money I may travel across the country. There is so much to see here.'

'Perhaps I'll go out to the West coast and dip my toes in the Pacific Ocean. I've heard that a lot of expatriate Britons live out there.'

A voice interrupted their reverie, making them jump. 'Is there anything to eat? I'm hungry!'

'Michael Byrne! What on earth are you doing, creeping up on us like that? I almost jumped out of my skin! And how can you be hungry? It's two o'clock in the morning!'

'My stomach doesn't think so. Can't I have a bit of that pork pie?'

'I was saving that for you to take back to the stable with you. Still, you might as well have it now as later, I suppose.'

Cait gave an enormous yawn. 'Hadn't we better get to sleep now, Mam? The pair of us will be like wet rags come morning. You don't want to be written up in the local newspaper as the bride who wore bags under her eyes!'

* * *

Morning dawned bright and clear. Cait helped her mother to dress in the neat blue suit and frilly white blouse she'd chosen as her wedding outfit. Cait had tried to persuade her to wear a smart frock, but Ruby had been adamant. The suit would be fine for wearing to church on Sundays, whereas the frock would hang in the closet from one month to the next, a wicked waste of money.

'I think that's it,' Ruby murmured,

taking a last look in the mirror to adjust her flowery hat. She had considered buying one of the new cloche types but had changed her mind on the grounds that it would go out of style before she got her money's worth from it. The local women wore head scarves for every day, and she would be doing the same.

Danny gave the bride away, and Cait was her sole attendant. Mickey had begged to be an usher, but that was hardly practical, so Ruby had gently refused. 'There won't be a single soul on the bride's side of the church, so we'd only look silly.'

'As for the congregation, they'll all be heading for their usual pews, so they certainly won't need showing to their seats. You sit in the front row, to give me a bit of support.'

By noon it was all over, and Ruby and Robert were man and wife. Everyone trooped down to the church basement, where the Willing Workers put on a delicious meal. Everything provided was much as it had been at the church social, except that this time Ruby was the centre of attention, rather than one of the cooks.

After the meal, there was a rush for the train. The newly-weds were off to Niagara Falls, that favourite destination of Canadian honeymooners. They were to drive to the station in the old mail buggy, which had been decorated with ribbons for the occasion. Someone had tied several old tin cans on the back, which clanked and rattled as the conveyance took off. It was lucky that steady old Brownie was pulling it, rather than Robert's sprightly mare. The noise was enough to spook a more nervous animal.

The train steamed in, and Ruby was helped up the steps, watched by the conductor, Ewan McPhail, who wore a sour expression on his face. Cait's expression, too, was solemn, as she took in the scene. Although she wished her mother every happiness, she knew that this was very much the end of an era.

From the last carriage, a young man climbed hesitantly down. He walked slowly towards Cait, who shrieked as she flew into his arms.

'Trevor! What are you doing here? Oh, I can't tell you how happy I am to see you! Why didn't you let me know you were coming?'

'I didn't write, in case you replied that you didn't want me. Your mam said you were seeing some chap called Martin.'

'I've never loved anyone but you,' she said simply, 'and I never will. Oh, Trevor! I thought I'd never see you again!'

'I had to come, my darling. I would never have been able to forgive myself if I had lost you forever.'

Suddenly, the sun broke through the clouds, shining down on the young couple but, as Trevor kissed his bride-to-be, they didn't notice.

We do hope that you have enjoyed reading this large print book.

Did you know that all of our titles are available for purchase?

We publish a wide range of high quality large print books including:
Romances, Mysteries, Classics
General Fiction
Non Fiction and Westerns

Special interest titles available in large print are:
The Little Oxford Dictionary
Music Book, Song Book
Hymn Book, Service Book

Also available from us courtesy of Oxford University Press:
Young Readers' Dictionary
(large print edition)
Young Readers' Thesaurus
(large print edition)

For further information or a free brochure, please contact us at:
Ulverscroft Large Print Books Ltd.,
The Green, Bradgate Road, Anstey,
Leicester, LE7 7FU, England.
Tel: (00 44) **0116 236 4325**
Fax: (00 44) **0116 234 0205**

FALLING LEAVES

Sheila Benton

When Richard employs Annie to update the computer system for his company, she finds herself, through circumstance, living in his house. Although they are attracted to each other, Richard's daughter, Katie, takes a dislike to her. Added to this, Annie suspects that Richard is in love with someone else, so she allows herself to be drawn to Steve, Richard's accountant. Annie feels she must choose between love and a career — how can the complications in her life be resolved . . . ?

ENCHANTED VOYAGE

Mavis Thomas

Lauren was a reluctant member of the family holiday group on a sea cruise, taking in Italy, Greece and Turkey. All her thoughts were of him: she agonised over Grant's accident, his operation, and his forthcoming marriage — to Elaine . . . However, whilst on the *Bella Italia,* Lauren became deeply involved with a charismatic member of the entertainment team . . . and a fellow passenger — a teacher and his two difficult children . . .

WHERE THE BLUEBELLS GROW WILD

Wendy Kremer

Stephen employs Sara, a landscape designer, to improve the appearance of the gardens of Knowles House, his Georgian mansion. He wants to use innovative ideas to generate additional sources of income and is hoping to hire it out for special events — an attractive garden would boost his chances. Lucy, Stephen's childhood friend, lives with her father on the adjoining country estate. Everyone thinks Lucy and Stephen are made for each other — but then along comes Sara . . .